John Saunders

Guy Waterman

Vol. 3

John Saunders

Guy Waterman
Vol. 3

ISBN/EAN: 9783337346645

Printed in Europe, USA, Canada, Australia, Japan

Cover: Foto ©Andreas Hilbeck / pixelio.de

More available books at **www.hansebooks.com**

GUY WATERMAN.

A Novel.

BY

JOHN SAUNDERS,

AUTHOR OF 'ABEL DRAKE'S WIFE,' ETC.

IN THREE VOLUMES.

VOL. III.

SECOND EDITION.

LONDON:

TINSLEY BROTHERS, 18, CATHERINE STREET,
STRAND.

1864.

LONDON: PRINTED BY W. CLOWES AND SONS, STAMFORD STREET,
AND CHARING CROSS.

CONTENTS OF VOL. III.

GUY WATERMAN.

CHAPTER I.

GETTING RID OF DISREPUTABLE CHARACTERS.

THE squire, Lucy, and Mrs. Hammett were sitting at the breakfast-table about a fortnight after the trial. They seemed all to be preoccupied, sad, and disinclined to talk. The squire was unusually fidgety; and more than once, when he heard an approaching step, got up, walked across the room towards the door as if to meet the footman, but took no further notice when he saw him come in with something for the breakfast. The squire then appeared to be engaged in stretching his limbs, as he said, after a bad night. Presently Lucy broke a long silence by asking, timidly,

'Is it not strange, uncle, the secretary of state does not answer the petition all this while?'

'Well—yes; we ought to have heard before this.'

'Do you think, uncle, there is any hope for him?'

'I do not.'

Lucy said no more for a little time, but the tears began to flow. The squire went on:—

'But, my dear, though at your request I consented to sign the petition, and though you were yourself so merciful as to forgive one of the greatest outrages that could be perpetrated on your feelings and character, even we, you know, could only ask for a commutation of his sentence, as the other petitioners did, on the ground of mercy. It was impossible to say he deserved a more lenient fate.'

'Oh! but uncle, is it not wrong to take life for anything but murder?'

'Well, I have had my doubts, I own; but I cannot also deny that I think such a man is far more wicked and far more dangerous than many murderers.'

'Oh! but, uncle, don't you think you might write again, still more urgently, before it is too late? Do, do, dear uncle!'

And Lucy, rising from her seat, stole to the squire's side, leaned upon his shoulder, and kissed him, while he, with some emotion, wound his arms round her waist. Still he said nothing, while he appeared strangely agitated and to be losing his ordinarily strong self-control.

The servant again entered with a folded newspaper in his hand. The squire put Lucy gently aside, rose and met the man, took the paper, and walked away to one of the windows to open and read it. As he turned, with the open sheet in his fingers, his face, which was generally of a ruddy, healthy hue in spite of his age, appeared so white that the bits of colour on the cheek that could not be driven off by any sudden emotion appeared like burning spots.

'My dear girl,' said he, 'all is over. I could not tell you till now that I did hear from the secretary of state that he had written to the judge to ask him whether it was possible to spare this wretched man's life, and that the judge's reply made it quite impossible while the law remained as it was. He—he died this morning, confessing his guilt and his shameless slander against you. Here! Mrs. Hammett!' suddenly cried the squire, interrupting his speech, 'she is fainting!' But no, Lucy did not quite faint, though for a time she seemed to pass through the valley of the shadow of death; and to experience such exquisite pain, physical and mental, that she sighed and wept bitterly to find herself again restored to her consciousness of a world that she had ceased to care for.

While she was slowly recovering herself, and trying to smile away the good squire's anxieties, as shown in his sympathetic face, the servant announced that Mr. Morgan was waiting in the little study. Mr. Dalrymple went to meet him.

'So, all is over with this miserable man, said the squire, as he stretched out his hand to Mr. Morgan, who sighed in answer, as he observed,

'It's a bad business, a bad business! First job of the kind I have ever had to deal with. Hope it'll be the last. But he gave us no choice. He was bent on his own destruction.' Mr. Morgan spoke thus, as if conscious he had himself been chiefly instrumental in making the squire adopt the sudden resolution to proceed against the criminal for forgery; and also, as if feeling (perhaps wisely) that some such thoughts were sure to be in his principal's mind, and therefore it was as well to have them out.

'Yes,' said the squire, after a long pause, 'tis a matter to make one review one's opinions on the humanity of our criminal procedure. Well, have you any fresh news?' Mr. Morgan put into the squire's hand the letter he had received from Mr. Pample in the gaol. The latter read with surprise the address,—'To be delivered unopened to John Sharker, Esq., if my life he happily spared; or, if otherwise, to Godfrey Dalrymple, Esq.' 'A complimentary association of names, certainly,' said the squire, looking at the letter very much as he might have looked at a toad that appeared in his way just when he was going to put his foot down. 'What have I to do with the thing?'

'I think you had better open it,' quietly remarked Mr. Morgan.

'If I must, I must.' So saying, the squire unclosed the packet and found four Bank of England notes for a hundred each.

'Just the sort of enclosure I expected,' said Mr. Morgan. 'Now I understand all. This is some of your money that Pample managed to secrete about him or get brought into the gaol; and he, no doubt, made the bargain with Sharker that he was to have the whole if he got him safely off so far as life was concerned, but, if not, you were to have it, as the real owner. A skilful stroke of policy! And Sharker did succeed, of course, easily enough, as he came to ask that which I was only too anxious to grant.'

'So that, in fact, Sharker has a kind of right?'

'Well, yes, for he offered to give up his client when he found that he refused to plead guilty; but I told him to do his best. But I have another communication for you.' Mr. Morgan handed the squire a letter in deep silence, and turned away while he read it. It ran thus:—

'*Condemned Cell.*'

'Sir,—Within a few hours after you receive this I and my crimes will no longer trouble the world. Can you now forgive me—you—and Miss Lucy Dalrymple? Oh, sir, *at last*, things assume their true value to me. I understand myself—what I have been—what I might have been. But I have no wish to darken your domestic peace with my black despair. I conjure you both to forgive me. I feel you will. I die in peace in that thought.

'I have already said to the sheriff and to the chaplain, who have been to see me, and who are very kind, that there was not one word of truth in my charges against you and the young lady. I repeat that here.

'May I ask yet one favour? The money in the letter which Mr. Morgan will give you is yours in a moral, perhaps legal, sense, but it was mine so far as that particular sum was concerned. I wish very much to have it divided among certain poor persons whom I have injured by my frauds, and whose names I enclose. I wish, too, a part to be given to Martin Galt. It was I who first persuaded him to be guilty of perjury, in order to save my life. I did him a kindness once and he remembered it. He blames Sharker, but I am, in truth, the most guilty party. What Sharker did he did at my suggestion. If you would, sir, kindly consent to this in consideration of my present unhappy state, you will only add another to the many obligations I owe you, and for which I have proved so ungrateful. Permit me, sir, to invoke Heaven's blessings on you and yours, and to wish you farewell.

'GEORGE PAMPLE.'

The tears were running down the furrows in the squire's aged face as he read on, and at the close his agitation almost overpowered him. After a while he said,

'Morgan, let everything be done as he wishes. What about Martin Galt?'

'Why, he will be tried, convicted, and perhaps heavily sentenced, unless this letter help him, which I think it may.'

'Well, do the best you can for him after the law has had its rights. Give him to understand that I

will help him to emigrate at the close of his im-
prisonment; or if he be sentenced to transportation
he shall not be forgotten in his banishment. And
as to Sharker?'

'Oh, the blackguard! he's off. He knew this
place would be too hot to hold him.'

'Very well. Mr. Morgan, this is and has been
in every way a painful business. I hope I and
mine have heard the last of it.'

'So far as I am concerned it shan't be again
mentioned, depend upon it, squire.'

And we, too, dismiss these characters from our
history, though we may probably yet have to deal
with some of the consequences of their actions in
relation to other persons, in whom, we hope, the
reader feels some interest, and noticeably in Phœbe,
Guy, and Lucy.

As to Lucy, the shock of the execution coming
upon the previous one, her unhappy love for Guy,
seemed to wreck her utterly. And for a time the
poor squire had a hard task to bring back anything
like the old domestic peace to the fireside of Branhape. But as soon as he saw her horror at Mr.

Pample's fate begin to moderate he proposed to her a visit for a few weeks to her father and mother; and that idea was successful. Lucy began to listen again to the squire's kindly wiles; Mrs. Hammett succeeded in making her smile at some gossip of the neighbourhood; and so at last they took her off in tolerably fair spirits to visit the doctor and his family. Lucy did not let the squire go without a word, a look, a pressure of fond arms, and a grateful kiss that told him he was not likely to be forgotten, or be esteemed as a gaoler when he should demand back his ' bird,' as he often called her.

But at parting, Lucy had something to say that she found it difficult to get out, and yet which she must say. But at last it came, in stammering accents, though with unfaltering purpose :

' Don't think, my dear uncle, I am insensible to your great kindness and delicacy in not speaking to me about—Guy.'

' Pooh, pooh, nonsense! I don't want to hear any more on the subject.' .

' No, uncle; but now I have begun I must go on and finish, and then we shall never have to talk about it any more—never, I hope, have to think about it any more. I want you, then, to know that I never for an instant dreamed of doing anything that could have hurt you. In fact, I—I hardly knew myself that I cared anything about him, except as one might for an old playmate, till it was too late for me to prevent feeling as I did. But even then I knew it could come to nothing—it must come to nothing. And if he had said one word, or done one thing, wrong towards you, I should not have hesitated—I should never have seen him again. But he did not. He suffered in silence, and anticipated all I could possibly have asked from him.'

'That's right, that's right! Guy's a fine fellow. I had no doubt of this in my own mind before you told me; but I am very, very glad to have it confirmed. Of course, his marriage settles all.'

'Oh, yes, indeed. I am not so weak, uncle, as to sacrifice either my own future or yours to a dream like this. I shall by degrees do what I ought; only if you see me a little depressed now and then, don't mind.'

'I won't, I won't.'

'And never, dear uncle, let us, if you please, mention the subject again. Guy is your steward; I shall act as though I saw in him only your steward; and then in a little while I shall cease to play the hypocrite.'

Lucy smiled as she said this, and gave the squire her hand, who, instead of shaking it as he would have done in his ordinary mood, and made her cry out, as he often did—'Oh, uncle!' from the fervency of the pressure, kissed it with so gallant an air that Lucy almost blushed, as she thought she saw before her a knight of the olden time, old in years, but young in spirit, and devoted to the worship of woman as a kind of earthly goddess. But as that episode and fit of heroism ended in a good laugh, Lucy said,

'Poor Phœbe! You will see how she gets on? She was greatly shaken by the trial.'

'Yes; but I am puzzled to account for her emotion at the end. She was just the woman whom I should have expected to have had but one feeling, that of triumph and exultation, at the conviction of one who had tried to injure her son and her son's friends. But there was always something about Phœbe I could not quite understand. I always wished to like her for my wife's sake; and for a kind of outspoken, downright sort of quality in her own character; but, whatever the reason, I never quite succeeded.'

'Oh, but women show things so differently. I have no doubt, uncle, she felt just what you say, but was overcome by her agitation, her illness, and the terrible fate of the guilty man.'

'Oh, no doubt; no doubt. I account for it myself in the same way. I shall see her as soon as I get home. I owe much to her, and will take care she sees I think so.'

One thing the squire did not confide to Lucy; that he had an additional motive for sending her away. He thought it best she should not be near Guy for the present, or, indeed, till after his marriage, which he determined to push on, if he could. And so they parted, little dreaming that they were never to meet again on earth.

CHAPTER II.

SUSANNA REWARDED AT LAST.

COULD Guy have forgotten, even for a short time, his secret trouble about Lucy, or have allayed his natural anxiety about his mother, who grew rapidly worse after the agitation of the trial, he would have enjoyed real happiness in his new position. It was in every way a source of interest and of healthy excitement; while its novelty and the wonderful improvement it wrought in his social condition stimulated all his powers into vivid strength. The squire saw this with extreme pleasure, for he felt that much of it was his own work; and he could not but note how tenderly and gratefully attached to him the young man was, in spite of the obstacles and prejudices that had of late years kept them apart; and as he noted this so his own heart began to answer it by an almost fatherly interest and affection. Not that either of them was in the slightest degree demonstrative. Each knew the other's feeling, so far as it was permitted to be known, by a kind of freemasonry of tones and unobtrusive acts, and by nothing more. Their daily procedure was somewhat of this kind :—Guy walked over to the Hall after breakfast (for he persisted in sleeping at home), and then he and the squire spent two or three hours in examining and settling accounts, answering letters, and discussing the affairs of the tenantry, the home farm, state of the funds, &c. When this was over, Guy mounted his horse and set off to carry into effect any special instructions he had received, visit the places where people were at work for the squire, or go off to Plackett if it were market-day, accompanied by the well-informed bailiff, to sell produce from the farm or consult the solicitors on legal business in hand. Conceive the freedom, the freshness, the delight of such a life to one so confined by poverty and circumstance as Guy had previously been! He could not at times believe it was true ; no, not even if he were at the time rattling along at a glorious pace through the green lanes; and feeling, in spite of his peculiar troubles, that he knew at last what it was to live.

He was thus galloping onward one afternoon across the common near to, but away from, his father's house when he saw a woman's figure not far off on her way back from the village. It was a very striking and graceful figure, and Guy knew it well; and, though his heart did not change its beat by the smallest increase of speed or his brain experience the least throb of pleasurable excitement, he went rapidly towards it, and pulled up so suddenly as to put Susanna in a great fright, which did not disturb her graceful attitudes or charming appeals for protection, and which ended in both of them giving a kind of half-laugh, though Guy's was followed by a more than half-sigh.

'Susanna, I have been thinking of what you said to me yesterday; and if I did not, in accordance with your desire, give you my decided answer then, I will now. I think you have acted nobly, and like yourself, in proposing to release me from my engagement; but you mustn't think I have hesitated a single instant about my acceptance of your offer. I understand you distinctly to say, do I not, that you do this for my sake, not your own? You have not changed in your—your feelings towards me?'

'Oh, Guy, how could you ask me that?' said Susanna, drooping her head, and turning away as if to wipe off, unseen, a tear.

'That's enough. If I had needed any other incentive than my pledged word you have given it to me. A kiss, and then I shall be off.' Guy stooped down from his horse to kiss the red lips, and away he went, to think once more with all his might of the business of forgetting Lucy. But he was again interrupted when he had gone but a little farther; he saw as he thought, and to his surprise, the squire in the distance on horseback coming towards him Of late Mr. Dalrymple had begun to yield to the exigencies of age, and confine himself very much to his house and an occasional stroll in his gardens. Guy turned a little out of his course, so as to meet him. When they met, the squire, seeing Guy's look of surprise, said—

' I am going to pay a visit or two in the village,

and, among the rest, one to your mother. I half
promised long ago to call upon her if she couldn't
come to me, and I hear she rather wishes it.'

Guy smiled, but said nothing ; though, as the
squire rode away he could not help inly asking,

' What can this mean, I wonder ? Is she worse ?'
His face darkened, his spirits sank, and he went the
rest of his journey in silence.

Let us look in upon Phœbe and see what this
request or wish of hers portends.

She lies on the old couch where for so many
months she has been accustomed to lie all through
the day, and is closely enveloped in shawls to
defend her from the increasing cold. She shivers
through them all, and looks almost appealingly
towards the bright golden sun, which is staring in
upon her through the window, and revealing with
unkind particularity every wrinkle in that careworn
face, the deathlike sallowness of the complexion,
and the pain of mind and body which is expressed
in the writhings of the mouth, and in the mournful
pathos of the once sparkling and happy eyes.

Susanna sits on a little stool by her feet, looking up at her with the fondest and most pitying glances, and holding constantly one of the thin, wasted hands.

'I must do it—I must do it—while there's time,' Phœbe murmurs, and Susanna looks up in surprise.

'Yes,' continues Phœbe, 'I've made up my mind, Susy dear, to tell you a great secret to-day; one that has well-nigh killed me. Oh, I shouldn't ha' been like this at my age if I—' But there she stopped, and for a time said no more. Susanna merely pressed her thin fingers within her own in an affectionate manner, and waited for Phœbe to speak again in her own good time. Did Susanna just then remember a certain deathbed at which she had assisted many years ago, when she had learned some valuable things, and been called by the same name—Susy, dear? If so, she must have determined to profit by her errors on that occasion and her great improvement since, for she was now evidently as careful as she had then been careless. Yes, certainly, Susanna is a very different person to Phœbe, her second 'mother,' from what she was to Susan Beck, her first.

'Susy, dear, I think you care a bit for me, don't you?'

'Oh, my dear, darling mother—care for you?' and Susanna's eyes began to gush.

'And you'd do what I told you, if I were to entrust very, very serious things to you?'

'What a base wretch I must be if I wouldn't!' exclaimed Susanna with some warmth. Phœbe smiled a little as she said,

'I didn't doubt you, Susy, dear; O no. Only, you see, one likes to feel sure; to hear you say what I can only think. Well, now listen to me, I couldn't ha' told you all this but for that dreadful trial-day. It frightened me more than I can tell you. But I want to say something about Guy and Miss Lucy. When I heard about them I began to fear you would have to give him up. But I didn't say anything to Guy, nor he to me, till last night, then he told me how you had said you would give him up.'

' And what did *he* say?' asked Susanna, naturally wishing to hear how Guy spoke on the subject to his mother.

'Why, that he thought he should now be able to feel towards you as a husband ought, and forget her.'

'Did he? oh did he say that?' and Susanna looked up to heaven in a kind of holy rapture.

'Yes, and that's partly why I made up my mind to tell you all. But first go to Stephen's workshop, put the big block against the wall that's on the side of the field, put it about the middle of the wall. Stand upon the block and reach as high as you can, and you'll find a very smooth and nicely-fitting brick that seems tighter in than the others, but it's loose and you can move it with a firm push.'

'You don't mean it's there?' exclaimed Susanna, incautiously, remembering how she had seen Phœbe take it away on that memorable sleep-walking night so many years ago, but forgetting that she ought to know nothing on the subject.

'I don't mean what's there?' said Phœbe, with a return of her old suspicion.

'The—the secret you were going to tell me?'

'Oh, well; yes, it is.'

Susanna marvelled, but was not again going to

risk being trapped, so looked up inquiringly in Phœbe's face, and said merely,

'Yes?'

'Well, go there, and bring me what you find behind the brick.'

Susanna leaped to her feet and was going off, when she was called.

'Susy, dear; be sure no one is nigh. Come back directly without it if Stephen or any of the neighbours are about.'

'Oh, I will take care of that,' said Susanna, who left the bedchamber with a quiet gait, but the instant she was out of Phœbe's sight clasped her two hands together upon her breast, and murmured, as she looked furtively round,

'At last! at last!'

She found the brick of course easily enough, and she got it out, and then she put in her hand to draw forth the long-hidden treasure—that treasure, that mystery, for which she had sighed and yearned night after night in her bed as she lay thinking of the hints her dying mother had given her about Guy's birth, and towards the recovery of which all

her words and actions, and, in a sense, all her
thoughts, had been devoted ever since. And now
here it was in her hand, a thick, dusty, little packet,
containing apparently a book, and possibly other
matters, such as letters. She turned it round—saw
the seal was sufficiently entire to prevent her opening
it without discovery, and then amused herself by
putting in and taking out the brick two or three
times, as if to satisfy herself that she could do it
quite easily and securely if she should wish it; if
she, for instance, might, for her own purposes, desire
still to keep in use the ingeniously-concealed
chamber. Having satisfied herself on these points,
she put the packet under the folds of her dress and
hurried back to Phœbe.

How Phœbe gazed on it when again that mysterious packet came into her view after so many
years! How much had she not already suffered
through it! How much more might she not have
to suffer, now that she was about to—

With trembling, skinny fingers she broke the seal,
removed the cover, and produced from it a letter,
also sealed, and a little pocket Bible, still fragrant

with the scent of the Russia leather in which it was bound.

'That letter,' said Phœbe to Susanna, ' must not be meddled with till it reaches its destination, which may be to-day, if I have courage to go on as I've begun.' She placed the letter by her side, on the couch, and took up the Bible. 'This was her Bible, and I was to give it to him.'

Who were the persons spoken of as 'her' and 'him?' Susanna panted to know, but she seemed only affectionately attentive to Phœbe—as though the latter's revelations were scarcely so interesting to Susanna as the question of Phœbe's own state and ability to bear so much excitement. There was a long pause before Phœbe spoke again. Sigh after sigh rose and passed away, and Susanna feared some unlucky circumstance might yet mar all her hopes, when Phœbe began to speak in a low, feeble, and hesitating voice, and it was noticeable that as she spoke she managed to make Susanna turn her head aside, so that she might not gaze on her face.

It was then that for the first and last time Phœbe told the story. She told it all through, holding

Susanna's hand, and speaking close to her ear in a broken, husky voice.

When she had finished, Susanna sat still, with her eyes looking down on the patchwork counterpane, musing. Phœbe lay back exhausted watching her, and in her own terrible excitement and wild remorse and fear, could not help wondering that the girl showed no horror, no natural indignation, at the story she had heard. But Susanna only sat still—musing.

' What about the Bible ? ' she asked presently, in a whisper.

' She gave it me, my lady gave it me when we parted, to give to her husband, and said, " If you give it with my boy he will understand what it means." Oh, Susy, what shall I do ? what shall I do ? ' she moaned. Susanna did not answer.

' I know what I ought to do, but oh, how shall I do it ? Did you see how the squire looked on the trial day ? Once when I was watching that poor wretched Pample, the thought came over me, " I've sinned worse than he, yet they're going to hang him ! What'll they do to me if—? " and then,

Susanna, he turned his face on me—the squire—all white and awful with anger, just as he'd taken it away from looking at that poor wretch, and then I thought I should ha' shrieked out before 'em all. What'll become o' me, Susy, my girl? How shall I tell him? Oh, how shall I tell him?'

'But why must you tell him?'

'Because I can't die and he not know! I can't die and Guy not righted! I can't, I can't!'

'Well, but, mother, darling, have you thought about Guy, what he will say and think?'

Phœbe groaned.

'Can't you manage some way,' continued Susanna, 'to take care that Guy shall be righted, and yet that you shall not see him look at you full of hatred?'

'O no, no; he won't do that—he can't do that! How dare you say he will do that?' Phœbe's voice rose high in her anger and distress.

'Hush, hush! there's a dear, suffering, darling mother. Say what you like, I won't change. But let me—only, darling, for your sake—show you how dreadful it will be if the squire should insist on dragging you to gaol.' Susanna stopped, for Phœbe had fallen back exhausted and faint, and it was some time before she was sufficiently recovered by Susanna's aid to pay any more attention. But when she did again feel herself a little stronger, she said, 'Prop me up, Susy, dear, while I write something in the Bible.'

Susanna did as she had been requested, then fetched pen and ink, and helped to support Phœbe while she wrote in a very tremulous character the following words :—

'Susanna knows all. In case I should not have the courage to confess what I have done before I die, and to right those that I have wronged, I have told her all, that she may make the truth known when I am dead, and show this, with the letter from my dead mistress, to Godfrey Dalrymple, squire of Branhape, whose forgiveness I shall pray for with my last breath.

'PHŒBE WATERMAN.'

Phœbe did not beg Guy's forgiveness. Did she intend to tell him? Or was she too proud, even at such a time, to acknowledge the true character of her position as regarded him ? '

Phœbe wrote the foregoing lines, not on the fly-leaf, but on the inner side of the thick cover of the Bible, so that it could not, like the flyleaf, be torn out. And she chose the place at the end of the Bible, on account of its being free from writing, while the corresponding place at the beginning had been used by Mrs. Dalrymple to write a few affectionate words concerning the gift to the child.

Susanna looked over Phœbe's shoulder and read the writing, and a gleam of sinister but joyous light burned for a moment in those blue eyes; but it was for one moment only, and the next she was quite absorbed in her care of poor Phœbe's aching body and still more aching heart.

' But I must do it, for all this ! He's coming !' exclaimed Phœbe, when the writing was done, and the packet made up into its former state and confided to Susanna's pocket.

' Who's coming ? ' asked Susanna.

' Why, the squire. I as good as asked him, through Mrs. Hammett, when she called here this morning, and I felt so ill that I thought I shouldn't live to see another starlit night through yon window.'

'Well,' said Susanna, 'I think it's very good of you to want to have it all known to the squire and to Guy, now that they cannot ever know it except through you; and when such a long time has passed; and when Guy and you have got to love one another so; and when there's so much less occasion, seeing that Guy and the squire are becoming great friends.'

'Oh, Susy dear, don't say any more! I want to think just like that; and I've been persuading myself to be quiet by just such arguments a many years, and—'

They were interrupted. A horse was heard to stop at the door.

'He's here,' said Susanna, gliding to the window. 'Yes, it is the squire.'

'Quick, Susy, quick; give me something—wine, brandy, anything—to keep life and courage in me for a bit, and then all will be over.'

Susanna poured out a glassful of strong brandy

—a thing never taken by Phœbe, who was remark-
ably abstemious, and Phœbe drank it off as if it
were so much water or milk.

'Bring him up, Susy, now.'

Susanna went downstairs, and presently returned
with the squire, who said, in his old, cheery voice,
as he got into the room, and seemed puzzled by his
own height and the low ceiling,

'Why, Phœbe, woman, this won't do.   Come,
come ; look up. Guy can't spare you yet. You
must benefit by his change of fortune. Why, you
ought to be ashamed of yourself—you, a young
woman, to fancy you are going to die, while I, a
hoary-headed old man, am daily plotting new con-
trivances to cheat Time and persuade myself I'm
going to live a dozen years longer.'

'Oh, sir !' Phœbe said, with an attempt to smile,
but tears came instead.

'Is there anything I can do for you ? I am sure
I shall be very glad. You rendered me a great
service, and I hope you won't think I considered
you paid off and done with because of that little
annuity.'

'Oh, sir!' again began Phœbe, but again the tears overpowered speech.

'Well, come, I think I understand. You are pleased at Guy's position; perhaps a little pleased with me for taking a fancy to him. There, I've said it for you; and now, are you content?'

'Yes, sir; yes, sir. You are too—too kind.'

Phœbe stopped, and gave up the vain attempt at confession she had persuaded herself she was about to make.

'There, then, good-by,' said the squire, holding out his hand, and taking hers in it with a kind of rough gentleness. 'You'll get better, depend upon it, now that your mind's relieved about circumstances and about Guy's future, which you may safely leave to himself and me.'

'Good-by, sir,' Phœbe murmured, in tones so inarticulate that the squire rather guessed than heard the words. He opened the door, and Susanna fell forward with her hands on the threshold, which was close to the top of the stairs.

'I beg pardon, sir; but the stairs are so dark,' murmured Susanna, looking very red in the face.

The squire laughed to see the poor girl's con-
fusion; but perhaps he might have had a different
feeling if he could have known that the pretty,
innocent-looking girl, whose fright so amused him,
had been really on the watch to break up his talk
with Phœbe by an ingenious surprise, if Phœbe had
stuck to her purpose, and begun to confess; or if
he could have been told the nature of the revelations
which Susanna had thus determined he should not
know—*yet.*

CHAPTER III

PICTURES IN THE FIRE.

WHEN Guy returned to the cottage on the evening of the day on which he had met, first the squire, and then Susanna, he found the kitchen or living room filled with neighbours, who were busily discussing, in a variety of tones and gestures, what was best to be done. There was also a smell of medicine about the place. The two facts spoke to Guy only too clearly as to his mother's state.

One of the more thoughtful among the neighbours, seeing Guy stand at the threshold irresolute, as if afraid to ask what had happened, hastened to allay his apprehensions by saying,

'Oh, she's better now.'

Guy heard no more; but, passing through the hushed and sympathetic crowd, went upstairs where he saw the poor thin figure stretched on the couch. He went and stood at her feet, and a strange pain shot through him as he looked at the pale face and staring eyes that seemed to see something awful in the whitewashed wall. Susanna was leaning over Phœbe. After a pause in which Guy seemed to become aware that his mother took no notice of his presence, he turned, went down the stairs, and said to the people assembled,

'Thanks for your help, neighbours; but I'm at home now, and we won't need to keep you any longer. I am very much indebted to you.' And then they all went away, some with a shake of the hand from Guy, and presently he was alone. As he was about to reascend the stairs, Susanna came down on tiptoe, and, putting her finger on her lip, said,

'Dear Guy, she's asleep, I think; we had better not disturb her.'

'But what has been the matter?'

'Why, dear, she was a good deal agitated about the squire coming, and she made me give her a whole glass of brandy; and it seemed, after he had gone, to throw her into a raging fever. Poor dear darling, she's been quite lightheaded; and she does talk such nonsense.'

'Well, Susanna, I will keep watch with her through the night.'

'No, no, dear; you are tired, and you have the squire to attend to, and—'

'What's the squire to me just now?' demanded Guy, almost savagely. 'I shall do as I say.'

'Very well, Guy dear; I have arranged everything so nicely. Stephen will sleep in my bed when he comes home, and then I can be with your mother in her room. She needs attentions that only one like me, who knows all her ways and wishes, can give; and she wished it too.'

'Did she?'

'O yes.'

'Well, then, I suppose it must be so. But I'll go up and sit with her an hour or two before I go to bed.'

So saying Guy went softly upstairs, and, taking the low stool, sat down by the couch and took Phœbe's hand. It was so cold and damp that the touch made him shiver. He saw that Susanna must have been wrong when she said his mother was asleep, unless, indeed, she had slept and waked again. She still kept staring at the wall in that dreadful vacant way, and presently she murmured in a hollow voice,

' Ask her what it is she's wanting of me. Haven't I done all I can now that it is so late ? Oh, Steenie ! Steenie ! tell her to keep her heavy wet hands off me. Make her go away. Stop ! No violence ! Draw the curtains, and I shan't see her, and perhaps she won't see me.'

Then she cowered low, her head falling on Guy's arm, and she lay still, looking apparently at something beyond him.

Guy looked over his shoulder and was surprised to see Susanna standing there. He thought he had been alone with his mother.

' It's strange,' he whispered to Susanna presently. ' She is asleep, I think, after all, though her eyes are open and she talks. But she has not once noticed me.'

' Yes, dear, it's very strange,' returned Susanna, letting her hand fall fondly on Guy's shoulder as

she stood over him. But Guy did not seem in
the mood for such familiarity.' He removed her
hand, let it fall, got up, and walked over to the
fireplace, where he stood, and looked back with
a grave, almost stern, face towards Phœbe, as
though he could for her sake almost battle with
Death himself. Susanna did not follow him, but
dropped down on the low stool he had left, and took
precisely his late attitude of holding Phœbe's hand,
and looking up at the poor invalid, whose wander-
ings of mind were now but too apparent.

Suddenly Phœbe cried out in sharp, high tones,

'Don't curse me? Oh, sir, haven't I brought him
up almost as well as you could ha' done? No, no,
don't curse me, or *he* will do it too! Would you
teach him that?'

'Susanna!' Susanna turned and saw Guy at the
door beckoning to her. She went to him, though
looking again and again at Phœbe as if to make
him aware it was hardly wise for her to leave the
couch.

'Susanna, you had better go downstairs. I would
rather you left us alone for a time.'

'Yes, but I think she'll be wanting me, poor thing! It's all coming back to her about her young days, and the sweetheart she had drowned at sea.'

Guy said nothing, but waited while Susanna moved about, smoothing the pillows, drawing the window-curtains, and doing half a dozen little things that seemed, in Guy's impatient, irritable state, to take up a great deal of time.

'Do, Susanna, make haste,' he said at last; and then Susanna once more quitted the room, whispering at the latest moment,

'The doctor said it would be best to let her sleep as much as possible. To get her quiet is the thing, he says.'

When Guy found himself alone again with his mother he was in an extraordinary state of agitation. Rumours had reached him from time to time that the neighbours were accustomed to say Mrs. Waterman had something on her mind; and that that was why she was always ill, without any particular disease to account for the illness. It was, no doubt, all nonsense, Guy had thought, or tried to think; but the moment one difficulty had been removed another seemed to start up. Why had she wished to see the squire? And why had she, after all, said nothing to him, or at least nothing of importance? For Guy had seen Mr. Dalrymple since the visit of the morning, and was quite sure from his manner that, whether Phœbe had confided anything to him or no, the squire obviously attached no sort of importance to the interview.

Again Phœbe began to speak, though the tones were so low that Guy could only catch here and there a word, out of which he found it impossible to shape a sentence. At last, however, he heard her say,

'Ay! but that letter, and that hair! I dare not burn them. Yet why shouldn't I? Who's to know, unless the sea gives up its dead?'

Should Guy speak to her—and conjure her to confide her trouble to him? He feared to alarm her if he suddenly brought her back to self-consciousness; and he felt also a kind of terrible fascination in listening to what might be the revelation of some evil-doing of his mother in the years long gone by.

Phœbe now sat up, rocking to and fro, as if

quieting a child. Presently she laid her hand on her forehead, and said, looking round at Guy, but with no sort of intelligence as to who he was in her eyes,

'Who is it said my boy was sick—dying? Look at him. See how strong he is—how beautiful! Does he look sick, Stephen Waterman, or dying, think you?'

As Guy's head hung close to Phœbe's, his hair almost touching her lips in his eager desire to hear and to understand what she was saying, Susanna came up to him once more and touched his arm:

'Your father's come home, and he wants to see you; and supper's ready.'

'Say I can't come.' But presently some new thoughts caused him, after a long look at Phœbe, and a briefer but curious one at Susanna, to add, 'Very well, I'll go down, while you watch here for a bit.'

As he went away, and Susanna softly closed the door after him, she stood for an instant as if smitten by a thought so serious and pressing in its nature that she forgot everything else—even where she was, or who was by her side. This was the tenor of her sudden reflections :—

' Has she said anything to him about the Bible, I wonder ? If he were to ask me for it and see what she has written, he will know all ! I might deny it if I were sure she didn't know what I was saying, but how can I be sure ? What a fool I was not to think of that sooner. Let me see. Yes. The gum I used in making up the wax flowers for my hair on my last birthday; there's some remaining, I think. I must see.' Susanna went to Phœbe, looked at her—at first in a loving and careful way, as if to be convinced of Phœbe's inability to judge of what was passing around her, and then in a hard and penetrating one—as if trying to get into the mystery of Phœbe's recent sayings and doings by means of her face ; and on the whole she seemed to be satisfied that nothing particular had happened since she had left Guy and his mother together. So she unclosed the door and slid down with her catlike steps to the lower room : and listened, as was her custom before going into a room, to learn if the conversation affected her or her interests.

What she heard did, indeed, give her fresh matter for thought:—

'Well, lad, it's a long while ago, and I don't think as I can remember much about it now except what everybody knows on.'

'Perhaps, father, you are like me, and scarcely know how much or how little you know till you try. I have a great fancy to-night to hear the story afresh. You can't do any good upstairs. Susanna and I and the doctor have done all that was possible. So don't be any more anxious than you can help. We must wait up, and it may serve to pass the time away.'

Susanna would willingly have stayed to hear all, but she had a powerful motive to restrain curiosity just then; and she knew that Guy could, after all, learn nothing from his father but what he knew or might have known before. So she stepped in, with a kind of sad smile on her face, saying,

'I ran down just to say that she's very quiet. I want to fetch something from my room, Guy, dear, before you go to bed.' And so saying, she went back again up the stairs to the upper story of the cottage. She soon found the gum-bottle. It seemed perfectly dry, and Susanna looked vexed.

'I can't make paste just now. Perhaps if I put some water it'll do; but then that'll make it thin. Well, I can do it better another time if I only get over to-night. Oh, if I only get over to-night! I don't believe she will live till morning. Then if she has said nothing, I shall know I am the lady of Branhape.'

Susanna went back to Phœbe's bedroom, who lay dozing in an agitated kind of slumber, starting at intervals, then crying out inarticulately, then wailing, then again at peace in sleep. Susanna went to the fire, took the kettle of hot water, and poured just a few drops from it into the little bottle. After a good deal of stirring and holding of the bottle to look at the solution, and feeling by the aid of a long and thick bodkin the consistency of the gum, Susanna paused as if to make sure that Phœbe, whose head was turned away, could not watch her subsequent operations.

'Though if she did,' thought Susanna, 'I'd tell

her I do it only to keep the secret from being known
accidentally — so that wouldn't matter.' She then
listened to hear if the conversation was going on
downstairs; and, after a moment or two, she distinctly caught the voices of both Stephen and Guy;
there was then no danger of Guy's sudden appearance
in the room. She then, putting her little bottle on
the bed, and turning her back to the door, so that
no one coming into the room could see what she
was about, took the packet from its place of deposit
among the folds of her dress, opened it, put the
letter on the bed; then, also putting the Bible on
the coverlet, she turned to the end of the book where
Phœbe had written. She saw there just one fly-leaf
of blank paper left by the binder. She carefully
touched this with the gum all round the edge on
one side, going over the paper again and again so
as to be sure that every portion, however minute,
was duly prepared, but so delicately that the line of
gum was scarcely perceptible to her own eyes; then
washing her hands, and wiping and drying them
very carefully, and holding the book so as to see
the natural position of the fly-leaf both when the

Bible was open and when closed, she allowed it to settle against the thick cover in the best position, thus entirely concealing the place where Phœbe had written the confession of her guilt. She then pressed the book close with all her strength, though keeping the pressure so steady that no movement of the contents could take place. She then opened the Bible, and wiped away with a fine cambric handkerchief the gum that had oozed out beyond the edge of the leaf, and looked anxiously to see if any trace was perceptible through the paper (which was thick, coarse, and soft) of the writing beneath. She held it in all sorts of ways to the fire and to the candle, and seemed to be quite convinced that no one would suppose that any leaf was there temporarily fastened, unless indeed they were examining the Bible with suspicious curiosity, which Susanna felt tolerably sure she could prevent. This done, the Bible and letter were replaced in the cover, and the whole in her pocket; and then, seeing Phœbe remained in the same unconscious state, she said to herself,

'Now to see if he gets anything from old

Waterman ;' and she went stealthily down to listen.

She perceived that Stephen was just finishing his narrative. After he had done there was for some time silence on both sides. Then Guy began to speak:

' Were the two babies at all alike ? '

' Oh, ay ; it used to be made a joke agen me that I didn't know which was which if it warn't for the fine clothes on the squire's baby.'

' Were there any marks upon either by which you could tell them for certain.'

' Not that I ever heard on. You best know if you've got any about you still that must ha' been born with you.'

Guy was again silent and thoughtful for a little while, as though his father's words raised no particular idea in his mind, and as if he had already passed mentally to some other part of the subject.

' Is there no living person — I mean except mother—who has seen anything of this—the death of the child at sea, or the parting between mother and Mrs. Dalrymple on the shipwreck ; — is there nobody ? '

'No, not as I knows on;' said Stephen Waterman, reflectively, 'and wasn't it a matter o' wonder that your mother and you should have lived and got through all them dangers, while the squire's lady, and the old ship, and all the crew went down to the bottom o' the sea? I always did think it a'most a miracle, and I do now. And I was thankful enough, you may be sure, when I see my wife and boy come back to me safe, and learned all that I've been telling on you now.'

'No doubt — of course you were.' And Guy again relapsed into silent thought.

'And was nothing ever heard of the boat's crew that escaped to shore with mother and me?'

'Never a word, my lad, as I knows on. The six men were seen going along the shore, half drownded, one after another, a rolling and stumbling, you know, like drunken men, in the direction o' their own ship—the "Marco Polo."'

'Then some of them may even yet live?'

'O' course they may; but, on the contrary, they may not. It's a long while since; and if so be as they do live, they're most like scattered abroad in all parts of the world. But what does it matter? They can't tell us any more—nor for that matter so much as your mother told everybody long ago.'

'No — no, that is true,' assented Guy, who seemed to feel himself wandering as in a maze, or as in sleep.

'It ain't no matter o' wonder,' Stephen remarked, 'as you takes a interest in the affair. I did once myself, and I couldn't help chattering about it all day with Darkley and the neighbours, and dreaming about it all night, till it regularly scared me; but somehow I forgot it at last, except when anybody made me tell 'em the whole business fresh over, just as I ha' told you to-night. I shouldn't wonder, now, but that poor wicked wretch who was hanged a while ago could ha' told you more partickeler.'

'Pample?'

'I mean what I say, Mr. Pample, the squire's old steward.'

'What did he know of the affair? You didn't mention him.'

'Didn't I, though. Well, not his name, perhaps

—but him it was, and no other, that the squire sent after the " Black Gull " to get the child back. Mistress Dalrymple was to be let go off if she chose ; but as for the child, why I've heerd as it was to have been worth Mr. Pample's place if he didn't bring him back somehow,'

'Yes? Go on.'

'Well, when he got aboard my lady shows her sperrit a bit at being followed in that way ; but when Mr. Pample see the child a-laying dead, just like, as he said, a poor white mummy in a case, just ready to be buried in the sea, he knew it was no use settin' up a to-do; so he left 'em alone, taking the dead child along with him, and brought it home ; and then, as I before told you, it was buried in the empty coffin of the squire's lady, whose body was never found.'

'Of course the captain and—the—the others on board couldn't have known he was coming?'

'Oh, bless you, no ; not till a few minutes or so of his coming aboard.'

'And then you say he found all prepared for the burial of the squire's baby ?'

'Yes; the captain was at the very time a reading the service when the men aboard Mr. Pample's boat hailed him.'

Guy smiled a strange smile as he again spoke, in a seemingly jesting mood, to his father; looking the while at him with a penetrating glance, and shrouding his own face with his hand,

'What a comical trick, father, they might have played the squire and Mr. Pample just then, if they'd been minded.'

'Eh? A comical trick? How boy? I don't know what you mean,' observed Stephen, looking as wise as he could, and trying hard to place himself for the moment on the level of the 'really clever lad,' as he often designated Guy.

'I was only thinking how the poor lady, if she had been still determined to take her son with her abroad and educate him as she pleased, might have suddenly imposed upon Pample by telling him the dead child was her own and the living one her nurse's.

'Why, that's what she and all of 'em did say.'

'Yes, father, I'm very stupid; getting sleepy, I

suppose.   I meant to say though I forgot to say it,
how comical it would have been to have done so, if
it had been the squire's chi.d that lived.'

'But it wasn't, or you wouldn't ha' been there
now, you know, to learn all these partickelers.
How could you?'

Guy didn't answer this. The maze seemed to
grow more and more confusing, the thick under-
wood more full of tangles, the paths more peopled
with shapes that laughed and made mock at him
while professing to guide him to the goal he was
trying to reach; and whence he might, in the
words of the poet, see as from a tower the end
of all.

'I suppose,' he resumed presently, 'Mr. Pample
never said anything to you about that scene on the
deck?'

'Ay, but he did though. He was a sociable,
kind sort o' man at that time, when he'd had a drop
too much, was Mr. Pample; and he liked to talk of
this journey of his, which they say gev' him more
than a little lift up in the world, by making him so
intimate with the squire; and once I recollects him

a telling me that he didn't trust to just seeing the dead child where it lay wrapped up, with only its face to be seen, but he undid the dead clothes, and there was the fine lace baby-things under 'em.'

'He told you that? He, himself, told you that, did he?' said Guy, with changing countenance.

'To be sure he did.'

'And he, himself, never said—I mean, he never seemed to doubt but that mother was right—had not been mistaken in any way in her notions of what had happened?'

'O' course not. How could he? And he was a sharp one, if ever there was one; but what could your mother or he have had to doubt about? Nobody could ha' supposed your mother could ha' robbed and murdered her mistress for the sake of the hundred pounds she brought home, and most on it for you. I don't see what else her worst enemy could have inwented. And then, as to mistakes, your mother was allus a very careful, good woman in important things; her head was allus a deal better than mine.'

'Thank you, father, I'm glad you've told me

this to-night, for it came to me almost as if I had never heard it before ; and I couldn't help, as you have seen, trying to look at the whole business as a stranger might.' Then he added, after a pause, in a low voice, ' because it so much interested me.' They now got up, and Susanna flew back to her post.

' What an ass I must have been,' said Guy to himself a moment or two later, as he went up the stairs to his mother, ' to have let my thoughts lead me such a wildgoose chase while he was talking. However, it's over, and I don't think he or anybody else will tempt me again to such work. I am glad he was so unsuspicious of what I was about. Poor father! he shames me, after all, by his natural and unbounded faith. He's content to know the simple truth and to stick to it with all his heart without further inquiry, while I—I—well, there, it's over ! I'm out of the maze at last.'

It was characteristic of Guy that, having once had his suspicions aroused and then effectually allayed, he threw them aside altogether, and felt only vexed with himself for having given way to such weakness. The consequence was that he no longer desired Susanna's absence from his mother's chamber. What could it matter to Susanna any more than to him how his mother raved, if there was no guilt in the ravings, no revelations in which he or others could have special and personal interest?

Susanna saw almost in the first minute of his return the change that had occurred, and inly congratulated herself, though it also brought another monition to her mind :

'I must take care,' said she to herself, 'that he doesn't now suspect me of wishing to keep him in the dark ; that would be worse than the actual discovery of what she can tell him. Yes, that might be a reason for his breaking his engagement with me ; whereas I can't be sure that he would break it even if he did discover his true birth, provided I hadn't provoked him by want of confidence. Yes, I must mind that.'

'How is she now?' asked Guy, putting his hand affectionately on Susanna's shoulder, and looking with new tenderness towards Phœbe.

'She keeps talking the same sad nonsense about all sorts of wonderful adventures. Do you know, Guy, I fancy that she remembers a deal of things she has read in novels long ago, and that it all seems to her like her own history.'

'I shouldn't wonder but you are right, Susanna. Mother hasn't often read such books; but I have always noticed that when she did read them, she could not help getting excited, as though feeling that the whole was a reality passing before her eyes.'

'Well now, dear, it is getting late. Hadn't you better leave her with me?'

'No, Susanna, not yet. You won't mind my keeping you up a bit longer?'

'Up! Why, Guy, dear, don't you suppose I am going to bed and leave the poor dear darling in that way?'

'Very well, then, if you don't object to my company, let me sit a bit longer. But don't mind me. I'll sit here in the chair by the fire, and perhaps even I may sleep. But, if so, be sure you wake me at the least sign of change.'

'Yes, I will.'

'And, Susanna, see if father is comfortable. Get him off to bed, if you can; he needs rest after his hard day's work. Do, and then come back, and we'll watch together.'

Susanna hesitated, as if not exactly liking this last commission, which might keep her away from the room a good while; but she fetched a low footstool for Guy, moved the chair into a more comfortable position, and stirred the fire; and then, when she had done all she could find to do for him, seemed to wait so sweetly patient for a kind word or gesture from him, that he could not but draw her to him and press an earnest kiss on her forehead, sighing almost imperceptibly as he did so. Then Susanna, with a sudden light of joy, as it were, upon her face, and with one—just one—loving, fond look towards Guy, who did not or would not notice it, went to the couch of the sufferer, kissed her, and, lastly, with a graceful flourish of the hand to Guy, went down to Stephen. Shortly after this, Guy was startled by the passionate outbreak that Phœbe gave way to, in a low but intense under-tone,

'It's done! It's done! I've got him away from her; we're in the boat. How it tosses. Oh, don't let it toss us both back to the deck. She how she waits holding out her arms. Oh, if she gets him back, she'll never again let him go. Never, never! Up and down, up and down! I think my brain grows giddy with this dreadful rocking. But, hush!—never mind, we are getting farther and farther away. Ha! what a light! Merciful heavens! did you listen to that dreadful clap of thunder? Is it all about my business, I wonder? What, all for taking away a little child—a living child—to replace my own dead one? Hush! how terrible it is, all this glare and noise! it seems to crash into my very brain!

'Yes, I can just see her, still looking after us; but how dark—how dark it grows! What is that man muttering—his prayers? Is there then danger? I must be ready; yes, ready for any difficulty. Am not I his mother now? Shall I not do all the fondest mother ever did or can? Oh, but I were wicked else. But I can: I will!

'Look, look! that wave—it comes! O God, save—save!

'Not dead! no ; let me but catch one breath—'

'Again light and air! Up, lift up the child!
What is this I-have caught? An oar? Oh, brave!
He will not die. I can save him.

'I grow faint! O God, how many more times
must I be overwhelmed by these horrible waves!
Yes—again they come!

'Ah! my foot touched the ground : we are safe!
Help! help! help! the child! I—I—.'

　　.　　　.　　　.　　　.　　　.　　　.　　　.

As Guy listened to all this—at first with incre-
dulity, then with awe, and then with a faith that
made the very hair of his head seem alive with
sympathetic horror at the glimpses of Phœbe's
struggle to save the child and herself from shipwreck, he rose to his feet, his head half turned
round to go away, but his feet rooted to the spot by
the violence of his emotions. Remembering, however, his recent experience, he determined to calm
himself, and to seek at another time for explanations
as to all he had heard—a time when he should be
in a more fitting mood to judge of them.

Phœbe was now quiet, with the exception of a

low, moaning sound, and Guy vainly waited, listening to hear if she would go on again. But she did not; and at last he dropped mechanically into his chair, and gazed into the fire.

He saw a picture there. A child was brought home by its nurse to the Hall. The squire received it into his arms as the last gift from his dead wife; and seemed to determine, as he gazed aside with tearful eyes at the portrait on the wall, to make up to the little one all the love and devotion he had failed to be able to show to the unfortunate mother.

The top of the fire broke, and with it went Guy's picture; but a new one came. He saw a happy, high-spirited boy, galloping along by the side of the proud squire towards the hunt, on a day of glorious sunshine and frost, with a host of red coats, and the musical clamour of a pack of hounds which formed a part of his picture.

Then again, as he kicked back a projecting red cinder into the grate, his picture changed, and he saw a youth in academic costume receiving the congratulations of his companions; he had carried off the highest honours.

But what is this new picture presented in that
eternal kaleidoscope, the fire, before him? Why
does he gaze so earnestly and longingly upon it?
There is but a single figure in it. Guy hardly
knows where it is supposed to be, or how surrounded.
It is enough for him that he sees what is ever to
man's eye the fairest object of creation, the one real
thing that contends for supremacy with the poet's
most inspired ideal—he sees there the woman of
his love, Lucy Dalrymple. But not long alone.
From behind the trees (for now the background be-
comes clearer) advances a young man, with all the
timid awkwardness of true, unspoken, unrecognized
passion, but with all the manliness of the true man,
not the less visible to her through the eyes, and
upon the brow, and on the lip. And they both
tremble as they touch hands; and then there is a
deep silence ; and then, in one word, one look, such
eloquence as never mortal ear listened to while only
playing the listener. Mutual love and consent are
exchanged—there is no obstacle—the squire's dearest object in life is to have that long secret desire of
his thus carried into effect.

But Guy's throbbing brain warns him he had better stop, at any cost, the procession of things passing through it, and shaping themselves as they go into these pictures of the fire, which show to him a history that might have been.

He rises from the chair, walks about the room, goes to the window and looks out. There other pictures wait him. He sees the distant fir plantations of Branhape; he sees that same babe—boy—collegian—affianced man walking through a thousand well-known paths; claiming every tree, every leaf, every blade of grass as his own; walking onward to the Hall, saying, ' This, too, is mine! ' Entering the vestibule, rich with marble and gilding, and acknowledging the salutation of the servants, who, with mingled affection and respect, seem to say to him, ' Welcome, oh, our master ! ' But still he goes on; for does he not know that all this sense of ownership is not quite true; that another master yet lives; and who, if that young stranger could will it, might live on for ever, so deep and passionate is the yearning love he feels for him—his father !

Guy turns from the window; for, like the fire, it seems bent on driving him mad. He looks everywhere, except in one direction which some inward monitor seems to bid him avoid. But at last he turns to *her*. He can resist no longer the overwhelming tide of growing conviction that Phœbe has not merely been raving. He determines to speak to her resolutely; he *will* know, once for all, if she be able to help him.

But even when thus resolved Guy paused to think how he might guard her against any sudden shock.

'What if I were to kill her by the vehemence of my words, and afterwards learn that it was all a delusion? Could I live as my mother's murderer?' So, struggling with himself, he came nearer to the couch, and saw Phœbe, to his surprise, looking quietly at him. But that was for a moment only. She raised herself on one arm and stared round the room in wonder, and then again looked at him, while he, feeling her eye upon him, endeavoured to meet her look with a smile upon his own face.

'Guy! Oh, Guy, my dear boy! Have I been very ill?'

'Yes.'

She put her hand to her head as if it pained her.

'I must have been dreaming. Have I been talking strangely?'

'Very strangely.'

Did Phœbe notice the unusual absence of the word mother—a word dear, very dear to her from Guy, for it was generally by that alone he expressed whatever of affection was passing in his heart towards her? Perhaps she did, for the old impatience seemed to come over her as she said a little irritably,

'Come nearer to me. There—sit down on the stool.'

Guy did so.

'Now kiss me, and say, "Mother, I forgive you if you—if you haven't been all to me you might have wished or ought to have been."'

Guy repeated the words after her with a tone the solemnity of which did not escape Phœbe. She suddenly murmured,

' Guy, I think I'm dying.'

' No, no ! '

' Yes, I think I am. You—you won't curse me
if—if you find I haven't been so good to you as
you may have fancied I was ? '

Guy could not answer; he could not speak,
there was such a choking in his throat.

' Guy,' said Phœbe again, and this time in a very
low and constrained voice, ' I want to tell you a
story.'

' Oh, Guy, dear ! ' interrupted Susanna, who
suddenly made her appearance, ' I am so frightened.
There's some one trying the shutters. Will you
just run down for a moment? '

' Susanna, mother is dying. Go to—to—my
father if you are in danger. She wants to speak to
me alone. Nay, pray go.' And so saying, Guy
fairly pushed the reluctant Susanna outside the
door, which he immediately bolted.

But this interruption had roused all the fiercer
and generally dormant elements of Guy's character
into unrestrained play. He no longer felt able to
listen to any protracted and circuitous statements

from the confessing criminal on the couch (as he now conceived Phœbe to be); for might she not be caught midway by death, and the secret, whatever it was, be lost for ever?

He went back to the couch and stood there for a moment gazing at Phœbe. She saw the change in his face, and her dull eyes seemed to shrink and close in anguish, while her own face became of a more deadly hue. And then he felt a great pang as if a dagger had been run through his heart. She would surely die and say nothing! Was she not shrinking back upon the couch as if conscious that her last moment had come? He must speak—he must act. With one knee on the couch, he grasped her arm, and said, in a low, hoarse voice,

'The story—quick! quick!'

But seeing she only shrank back the more, with ever-increasing alarm at his aspect, and that she was altogether failing in strength, he cried, in tones trembling with passion,

'Mother! mother! don't leave me like this!'
And then, quitting his grasp, he raised his hand

towards Heaven, and said, 'Before God, to whom you are fast going, answer me, *Are you my mother?*'

She did not answer him, did not breathe; did nothing but look at him with a gathering film visible upon the once bright, glad eye. Again he gripped her arm and bent over her, and fixed his eyes on her face as if he would keep her against death—against everything—almost, in his fury, against God—till she answered him. But seconds, minutes, went by, and neither moved a muscle. The white face grew drawn and fixed, and the tears that had come recently into the eyes seemed to freeze there. At last he dropped the arm, and the clenched hand fell with a heavy dead knock on the woodwork of the couch.

Phœbe was dead.

Guy knew it, and in his madness at being thus shut out of the secret for ever, could have shouted to the poor weary spirit that was turning at last to its earthly rest to come back and give him justice and amends. But he knew that all this passion was henceforward folly. She was gone—she had not spoken. He must remain as he was, no matter what rights he might have, what precious relationships he was entitled by nature to claim.

He forgot to call Susanna and his father, but there was no need. Before he could have supposed they knew, he saw them both standing in the room.

Not caring to witness his father's grief, feeling a new gulf between them, yet ashamed of himself for allowing his natural affections to be poisoned, he merely grasped Stephen's hand in silence, wrung it warmly, went downstairs, and hurried forth into the midnight air and darkness.

How or where he wandered that night he scarcely knew afterwards. A stream here and a bridge there seemed to connect itself with the eventful hours in his memory; but that was all he could recollect. On and on he went, mile after mile, hour after hour till at last, just at daybreak, he seemed to discover that he was thoroughly exhausted, body and mind, and must go home.

And then he returned. At first he went up to his bed; but he found it impossible to sleep, except by snatches of a minute or two, although so fatigued But in these short, fitful sleeps Phœbe's image seemed to pursue him ceaselessly, with streaming eyes and anguished face, saying nothing, but looking at him whenever he would look at her, with such tender and passionate reproach that he could not bear it. Then after a while it seemed to murmur, in tones of inexpressible sadness,

'Have I not loved you? Did ever true mother love you more tenderly than I have done? My crime—was it not that I might possess you, whom I had nursed from the very hour of your birth? Was not my blood a part of you? O Guy—Guy—Guy! Will you deny me now? Doomed of God and of man, I have you only. Will you desert me now and for ever?'

Guy leaped suddenly up from the bed—he had not undressed—and he went to his door to listen. All was still. The neighbours had done their kindly offices to the corpse and gone away. Stephen was in the living room below in the arm-chair by the fire, weeping like a child. Susanna was also abed, by no means weeping, for she was, on the whole, rather inclined to laugh, for she knew she had succeeded. So Guy heard nothing as he listened but the chirp of early birds just awakening.

He stole down the stairs without his shoes to the first landing, and entered the chamber of the dead. He started to see *that something* lying along the couch, the form of which he could so distinctly trace under the large black shawl which had been carefully disposed over the whole of the dead body. He lifted the shawl at one end, and there was Phœbe's face almost with a smile upon it, as if conscious he had come in answer to the prayers of her apparition. Guy gazed a long while, then stooped down and kissed the clay-cold lips, and then his heart gave way. He forgot all the crime—all the loss; and he remembered only her great love for him and his own exceeding love for her. He wept bitterly.

He moved not for a long while. He looked at the mouth that had so often kissed him, and sung to him, and taught him to be an honest and independent man; and to the bony hand that had worked for him for so many years; and he found every angry thought melt away, to return perhaps at some future time, but not now. And he could only wonder at the love that had dared so much and suffered so much to make him her own. Again he kissed the cold lips, and murmured—

'If thou canst yet hear me, listen. With all my heart and soul do I forgive thee.'

Was it the roseate hue of the dawn that suddenly threw so fair a gleam across the sleeper in death, and gave almost a kind of lifelike expression to the constant smile? Guy looked round in awe and wonder through the window upon the beautiful sky, but again turned to the couch.

Yes, he was Phœbe's boy again, and she was his mother—his own mother in love—and she lay there dead! And there was a fearful trouble upon her soul, even now as she stood before her Maker. He knelt down and kissed the grey hair on the pillow, and wept over it. He buried his face on her breast, and stretched his arms over her, and almost could have cried, as in his boyish days when he had any great grief, 'Mother, take me!'

But Guy was strong, and he soon obtained the master hand of his passion, and held it down. Then, folding his hands together and shutting his eyes, he tried to fancy he was with her in heaven, pleading her cause, as he said,

'Master, take the burden from the weak workman and lay it on the strong! Take her debts from her, and make me debtor of them.'

Poor Guy! he little knew how soon or how fearfully Phœbe's wrong-doing would be visited on him when he asked this.

He did not rise from his knees, but stretched himself wearily down by the couch, and drew a corner of Phœbe's old shawl over him, and the two slept peacefully side by side in the quiet morning twilight, the living and the dead.

CHAPTER IV.

WHILE GUY SLEEPS.

Not long after Guy had fallen asleep by the dead body of Phœbe, the door began to move by almost insensible degrees, an inch or so at a time, getting gradually more and more open, until at last a form appeared on the threshold, itself making just the same kind of guarded, noiseless movements while advancing into the room. Then, after a long pause, looking the while fixedly at the black shawl —not at the dead woman lying hidden beneath, but at the living man, also hidden by the shawl—the form advanced, and went, gliding rather than walking, to a corner of the room where stood the antique chest belonging to the deceased woman, and which has been previously mentioned in these pages as Phœbe's favourite place of deposit for her valuables. Susanna—for she it was—knelt there, and drew from her pocket a bunch of keys, keeping them carefully divided by means of her fingers so that they should not clink, while she watched with head half-turned round every movement of the black shawl made by the breathing of the sleeper.

Presently she began to push one of the keys into the lock, taking a long time over it, till she found it would go no further, and then she began to turn it round till she felt the resistance of the bolt. Then she paused, again looked towards Guy, drew in and almost seemed to bite her lip, as if admonishing the bolt to silence while she forced it back; then, with eyes fixed on the sleeper, she made, with sudden decisiveness, the inevitable turn of the key. There was, as she had feared there would be (for Susanna had often heard the sound before), a sharp, strong click, and so far she was disappointed in her hope, that by a skilful touch, she would evade all noise. The limbs of the sleeper moved, the corner of the shawl was pushed aside, and Susanna stood staring in affright, expecting the next instant to see Guy's head turn towards the place where she knelt. But he was not awake. Something between a sigh and a moan escaped him, and that was all: he again became quiet; he was evidently asleep.

Susanna smiled that pecular smile of hers which was at once so full of enjoyment for herself, and yet so dangerously significant as to others, that she never ventured to indulge in it by any chance except when alone. Susanna smiled as she turned away and raised the lid of the trunk, and began busily to explore the contents. She soon brought forth a sheet of letter-paper on which was some writing. She just glanced at it and again smiled. She had evidently obtained what she came for. Without pausing to read the writing she hurriedly folded up the paper and thrust it into her bosom, still jealously fastening her eyes the while upon Guy's slightest movement in sleep.

Rising from her knees, as if to be ready to seem engaged in quite other business if she should now arouse him, she gently shut down the lid; and then with one skilful and rapid touch turned the key and drew it out, and had the whole bunch in her pocket before Guy could have noticed anything, even if aroused by the second clicking of the bolt. But it seems to be a peculiarity of sleep that we get accustomed to noises, and so are less and less disturbed by their repetition. This time Guy heard nothing, and slumbered on in his melancholy and dreamy slumber.

Quitting the chamber with much greater expedition than she had entered it, though still with a step as noiseless as that of the ghostly shapes which are said to be driven off by cock-crow, and taking care to close the door after her, Susanna slid down the stairs to the lower room, where Stephen was sitting in the armchair, bent almost double, having evidently cried himself off in his grief like a child. Susanna drew close to the table, and pushed the keys (which she still managed to keep apart) along the table, close to Stephen's hands; evidently intending he should find them just where he had put them, and be unsuspicious of their having been touched. Again Susanna smiled as she saw the keys safe, and looked down upon that broad, rounded back and sleeping form doubled up in what seemed to her such a comical fashion. A minute later and Susanna was sitting on her own bed, upstairs, holding the stolen sheet of paper before her, and saying to herself,

'I wonder what my clever mother would say to this? That I should have guessed there might be such a paper; that I should know where it would be, if anywhere; that I should have got the keys from one person without his suspecting me, and opened the trunk and found my prize in the presence of another, and he the very one of all the people in the world who would most like to have caught me and my prize! Let me see what it's all about. "*Sunday, Dear Guy.*" But she had written, I see, "*My own darling boy,*" and then rubbed it out and put only "*Dear Guy.*" I'm afraid I shan't be able to make it all clear, it's so altered and scratched, and the ink has run in so many places, I suppose with her crying. Well, I must try, though I know well enough what it was written for, or I wouldn't have ventured so much to get it before anyone else might know of its existence. So now for another try.

' " *Sunday.*

' " *Dear Guy,—I have told Susanna a dreadful secret* ['Oh, of course! I knew what she was up to,' interjected Susanna], *a secret that I meant to have told to you and to the squire; but I am too cowardly, even now that I know death is coming, to risk seeing you look at me as at an enemy, and to hear the squire tell all the world that I am infamous. But I have told Susanna everything. I rely upon her to do all that can now be done to induce you to forgive your poor nurse* (the word *mother* had been scratched out and *nurse* substituted). *Susanna is to be your wife. She knows that you are too noble to run from your plighted word, since you have given it to marry her. I cannot, therefore, doubt, and I do not doubt, that she will act rightly by us all. But I feel I must leave nothing now to chance or to the possibility of others doing to me as I have done to my poor injured mistress. I shall, therefore, unknown to her* [Susanna stopped, looked at the opposite wall and laughed; then, after a pause, smoothed out the letter with an air of extreme content, and went on], *write a bit at a time, as well as I can, the whole story of your birth and of my guilt.*" But there the paper ended.

'I wonder why she didn't go on?' mused Susanna, as she held the paper to the candle and watched it burn away. 'Oh, I see! of course! I watched her so closely she couldn't. And besides she knew she had said enough here to make me tell all the rest. Yes, I must have spoken out if Guy had got hold of this, and then I must have persuaded him as well as I could of the excellent motives that kept me quiet before.

'I'll be bound he goes hunting her things all over as soon as he wakes. He must suspect something now about himself. Well, he may hunt to his heart's content. I shall go to sleep myself at last.' And Susanna, smiling at her face in the glass, began to undress, saying as she did so,

'I hope those nasty cocks will give over soon. How they do seem to be waking one another up all over the country?'

CHAPTER V.

SUSANNA had, with her usual penetration into all the superficial phenomena of human motive, rightly guessed as to Guy's action when he waked an hour or two after Susanna's stealthy visit to the chamber. The first whirl of emotion had then passed away, and his brain had ceased to be giddy. He looked round with surprise to see where he was, rose slowly to his feet, saw the veiled figure, and shuddered to think he had been so long with and so close to the dead. He drew back the shawl and looked on the white, death-smitten face, which still seemed to look sweetly back upon the world it had left for ever, then, as he replaced the shawl, he murmured,

' Poor creature! I do believe she meant to tell me, but was unable either because of her fear or from sheer physical inability. But is it possible,' he suddenly asked himself, 'that she would allow herself to draw so near to death without some kind of written record being ready, unless, indeed, she had found a simpler and a living record in Susanna? Can Susanna know? Or, if she has been told, does she disbelieve, and so hesitates to tell me what she thinks may only unsettle me for life, because unprovable? But no; if Susanna does know she must have proofs; they would be sure to accompany a confession. And then, she ought not to have lost a moment in telling me. Nay, she could not honestly. Pooh! this is all idle. She does not know. Of course, the idea of such a future for herself would make her—would make any woman —burst into speech. I shall learn soon what she knows or thinks; but, meantime, I may dismiss as a dream the idea of help from Susanna.'

'But has not my '—here Guy paused a little, as if hesitating alike to use or to refuse the word that presented itself—'mother—has *she* not put by somewhere all that I can desire to know?' Guy stopped a moment or two in thought, then went downstairs to Stephen, who was still asleep, with the keys lying before him on the table where they had been left by Phœbe. Guy took them, and was about to wake Stephen but altered his mind and went upstairs alone. He first examined the trunk. There were many things that would have interested Guy a few years back, but nothing that now engaged his notice for a single moment till he got to the bottom of the box. There he found a little pair of white woollen socks, with a label pinned to them, on which he read, in faded characters—'He wore these when I saved him from the storm.' With nervous fingers Guy handled the tiny coverings of his own baby feet, and drew from the sight of them a conviction that he could not have mistaken the character of Phœbe's revelations the preceding night. The chief incident of the storm which he had heard so vividly recalled by the delirious patient was, then, no trick of a feverish imagination. A child had been saved in the eventful manner described, and no doubt the guilty circumstances that weighed so heavily on the soul of the self-accusing and dying woman were also real. But Guy wanted proof, not conviction, which he already had; and this was nowhere forthcoming. In vain he turned over and over the contents of the trunk, in vain examined every box, every cupboard, every article of Phœbe's clothing, her pockets, her drawers, her shelves. In vain he turned back the bed (an old hiding-place of Phœbe) in quest of some letter, or book, or document that should satisfy the craving for proof that now possessed him. After he had spent more than an hour in this way, he stopped, saying, with a tone and look of intense despair,

' No, there is nothing! She has died, and made no sign. Well, God forgive her, as I have done; for she needs forgiveness! '

That was the one bitter thing that Guy said about Phœbe, and it was the last time he allowed himself so to speak.

When Susanna and he met at breakfast, Stephen had gone to Guy's bed, feeling chilled and ill after his sleep in the kitchen. Guy thought to himself that, if Susanna said nothing, he would question her as to her knowledge. But he hesitated when he found she not only said nothing, but looked as if it were

quite impossible she could have any great mystery
to talk about; for was he not exposing his own
secret belief by such attempts? However, when
Susanna had tried two or three times to make him
talk, he asked suddenly,

'Susanna, did mother say anything—particular—
to you before she died—when she found she was
getting so ill?'

'Why, yes, Guy dear, she did,' replied Susanna,
with a kind of maidenly shame in her manner and
a growing blush on her cheek, which she evidently
tried to hide from Guy.

'What was it?' eagerly demanded Guy.

'I don't like to tell you.'

'Pooh, nonsense! Don't be a child! Speak!
speak!'

The last word was said almost sternly, and
Susanna's face became overcast, and she pouted,
and seemed about to cry, as she said,

'We oughtn't to talk about it now.'

'What do you mean, Susanna? I have never
yet been angry with you I think.—not, I mean,
since we have been engaged; but I shall be angry

if you behave in this absurd way. You see me
agitated — see me eaten up with anxiety — and
yet—'

' Don't, Guy dear, don't look like that, and I will
tell you, though I can't bear to do it. She—
she—said I was to be sure to tell you that we—
we—we—' here Susanna began to sob—' must not
put off our marriage long on account of her; for—
for—she said it wouldn't be right we two living
together in one house, and no mother. There, Guy
dear, now you know; and I wish I'd bitten my
tongue off before you'd made me tell you—with
the poor dear darling lying dead upstairs.'

' That's all?' said Guy, with a sickening look
of disappointment.

' What else could there be, Guy dear?' asked
Susanna, trembling inwardly lest she might now
find that he did know that she knew, and that she
would have to resort to her boldest inventions to
get safely off while acknowledging the truth.
But, as soon as she dared to look at him after thus
speaking, she was reassured by his face. He could
not thus look if he was thinking of her conduct.

No; he was simply in despair that Susanna was not able, as it appeared, to confirm his secret hope. From that moment Susanna trod the ground with an airy confidence, that was in itself sufficient to remove all suspicion of double-dealing, even if such a thought for an instant crossed Guy's mind.

He asked Susanna no more questions. She had, it must be confessed, answered his first one too skilfully to tempt curiosity any further.

CHAPTER VI.

GUY PICTURE-STUDYING AGAIN.

Two days after the funeral Guy returned to his
duties at the Hall, looking so haggard and with
such an aspect of sudden age upon him, that the
squire, when he met him in the Hall and shook
him by the hand, could not help saying, somewhat
reprovingly,

'Come, come, Guy lad, you mustn't give way.
'Tisn't as though you hadn't long expected it, or
even as though you had any reason for anticipating
her return to health and spirits had she lived.'

Guy murmured something in answer, he scarce
knew what; he felt pained and humiliated at being
supposed to be suffering exclusively for Phœbe's
death; he knew only too well that, with his real
grief for her, there mingled personal reasons and
motives of a very different character.

'Come, business will do you good just now, and me too,' added the squire, 'for I begin to miss you.'

Guy looked up, and, as his eye met the squire's friendly glance, he felt a sudden lightening of his trouble, and he smiled as he said,

'I hope, sir, now to make up for lost time.'

'Well, you'll find a batch of papers in my little study, chiefly letters that want answering. I've been trying to get through them myself, but somehow I begin to perceive a fact that is always, I suppose, hard at first to realize—that I am growing older every day.' The squire smiled a melancholy smile; and Guy would have given worlds to have been able to contradict the fact, if only he had known how. 'Go there and begin, and I'll come to you when I've dismissed the visitor who has just called.'

Guy went as directed to the little study; but before he could see the papers, or give a single thought to the duty he had come to perform, he had caught a glimpse of the portrait of Mrs. Dalrymple, which seemed actually waiting for him as

he entered—waiting as if the subject of it were
expecting him to greet, to speak to her. Strange,
he had only the day before gazed on her empty
coffin in the vault (whither he had gone with Joshua),
and filled it in fancy with its proper occupant by the
aid of this very picture, which he remembered most
accurately, since the night of his confinement at the
Hall. He had not sought that gloomy communion
in the vault for its own sake, but in order to learn
from Joshua, without exciting his suspicions, if Phœbe
had done anything during her visit to it that might
justify or disprove his secret speculations. He had
learned nothing new. But he had been brought
in spirit face to face with her to whom he believed
he owed life, and into personal connection with
the dusty but splendid mementoes of his ancestry.
After a night's rest he had put aside all the disturbing influences thus thrust upon him; and now,
the very instant he returns to the every-day work
of life, it is she who confronts him—who draws his
eye, heart, and soul towards her, crying to him in
a language only too eloquent for him to bear, 'Art
thou come to me at last?'

In vain he tries to take up and read the docu-
ments before him. That soft, tender eye is ever
upon him — seems to reproach him for his own
averted face—suggests to him he must be without
strength or manliness to submit to eternal banishment from his own kindred. But what can he do?
Has he not already asked himself that question
a hundred times since the night of Phœbe's unconscious revelations and death. How is he—a
young man known to everybody as of humble birth,
whose whole life has been spent under the eyes of
the village residents, who has by circumstances of
special good-fortune been able to win the countenance of the great man of the neighbourhood,
and been thus lifted up out of his own natural
sphere—how is he, this young man, with so many
motives for delicacy and gratitude, now to come
forward, as if basely trading on the very kindness
shown to him, and say, 'This is not enough: I
claim to be the son of this gentleman, the heir to
these estates?' And on what foundation? The
dying and delirious words of his reputed mother,
who, in a kind of dream, while again agitated by

the recollection of all the terrible circumstances of
the storm which had drowned her mistress and
wrecked herself with her supposed child, lets drop
a few words about her guilt, and to the effect that
she had imposed on everyone by bringing home
the squire's child as her own, when the latter had
been wrongly supposed to have died on the vessel.
This was all. Just a few random words, heard
only by himself; and on this foundation he was to
condemn to infamy the good name of his supposed
mother, and claim alliance with the squire—a claim
that could only be received as the act of a madman
or of a rogue!

Was he not, in fact, exposing himself to the
imputation of being no longer of healthy mind?
Had he not all these last few days been nursing
a delusion, that he ought to have put down at once
and for ever the moment he became aware of its
existence? How easy it was to give in to such
a delusion! How pleasant! Not that Guy feared
for himself or his motives in a mere worldly point
of view. He laughed to scorn, as he well might,
the idea of being drawn on into this interminable

maze by the thirst for wealth, lands, or social position. He was perfectly sound there. But what he could not be so sure about was the precise effect on his judgment of the temptations held out by the thought, 'This man, whom I have always loved and revered more than any other man in the world—ay, even when he seemed most harsh to me, most distant to me—this man is, perhaps, my father!' It did stir the blood in his body but to think of that. He could not help it. And he feared that such thoughts might have within them a tendency to try to realize a false success.

And then again, when he asked himself, 'Is this lady my own true mother?—is it for me these sweet, affectionate eyes have so often rained down tears of joy and sorrow, of hope and alarm?'—Guy could not but be influenced by his own question. It might be weakness, might be lack of healthy self-control, might be the desire to escape from the many humiliations that will cling about the family history of the poor; but, whatever the cause, he could not now look upon that picture, gaze into those dear eyes, commune with that tender heart.

without feeling new instincts, new affections, almost
new powers, budding in his soul, as if in sympathy
with *her* nature, as if obedient to some over-
mastering sway of the mystic relations of blood.

He went towards the picture, no longer able to
repress his agitation. He stood before it, and
looked at it in passionate silence. At last he
threw up his hands to his head, which he had already thrown back; he pressed them convulsively
against his face to keep in the oozing tears, as he
murmured,

'Oh, my God, tell me the truth, and let me
rest!'

CHAPTER VII.

SUSANNA had waited with patience through all the days of the funeral for some sign that her ingenuity had not been thrown away in making Phœbe, from her death-bed, recommend Guy to think of an early marriage. But the sign had not come. Guy had met her at meals often without exchanging a word beyond the most necessary expression of his wishes, or the answers he was compelled to give to questions Susanna put. But his taciturnity might mean nothing more than grief for the loss of his mother; or it might mean that he had caught some inkling of the great secret that environed him like an impenetrable cloud: a supposition that did not at all alarm Susanna, so long as it did not also involve hostile influences with regard to her marriage with him. But as soon as the funeral should be over that

young lady haJ determined in her inmost thoughts
she would have a better understanding, or learn
very good reasons indeed why she should not.

The funeral is over; and Guy having been, as we
have seen, to resume his duties at the Hall for the first
time since Phœbe's death, came back from the Hall
so late last night that Susanna, who had long waited
for his return home, had given him up and gone to
bed, convinced he was shunning her, yet determined,
when they should meet at breakfast, to try once more
her native cunning in dealing with the difficulties
that her wayward lover continued to throw in the
way.   It is a fine autumnal morning; there is a
white mist in the air ; and the floating spiders' webs
are stretching from pale to pale, and from tree to
tree, swaying to and fro in the air as if wondering where they shall next fasten themselves.
Susanna, who has seen that everything is prepared
for Guy's breakfast, and has already two or three
times boxed the ears of the little servant-maid
(whom she has recently engaged) for not perfectly
understanding what Susanna had forgotten to explain—Susanna, having seen all ready, and finding

Guy still delaying in bed or in his chamber, walks
out to the garden, then to the workshop, as if drawn
by a secret desire to make sure that the precious
book and letter are still safe where she had again
recently deposited them in Phœbe's hiding-place.
A glance at the brick which closed the aperture
satisfies her all is right. Yet she lingers, looking about her, and her thoughts shape themselves
in half-uttered words, thus :—

'I wish I knew how to make Stephen keep away
from this place. He may be bringing people in,
and nobody knows what may happen when I'am not
here to watch. I'll tell him I saw a ghost coming
out at daybreak the very morning of his wife's death.
I know that'll frighten him a bit. And he shan't
keep an extra key. I'll hide the one Guy used to
have and say it's lost ; and the other I'll hang up
just where it can be reached through a broken pane.
But then there isn't a broken pane ! And it musn't
seem done on purpose. Oh, I know ! I'll break one.
Is there a nail in a good place ? Yes, here's one,
just within reach, I think ; and where nobody outside who didn't know could suspect the key being

there, even if they put their hand in and felt about. Yes, I'll do it all just as naturally as if it had happened by accident.'

So saying, Susanna went out, locked the door, and after a sharp glance all about her, which she disguised under a show of interest in the floating spiders' webs, and in the 'pretty' spotted, light-coloured insects who were so busily weaving them, took up a stone, and, going near enough to the window to be sure of her mark, threw it. The glass crashed, and the stone went through and fell on Stephen's bench; but the breach made was not exactly to Susanna's taste. The hole was large enough, certainly, for a hand and arm to go through, but then the edges were so jagged, and stuck out in so many threatening, sharp-pointed peaks, that Susanna did not at all like the idea of trusting her fair soft hand and arm through such a dangerous pass. But, after a pause, she smiled and said to herself,

'All the better. It's only for Stephen and me, and the less he comes the better I shall like it. Now, then, to try if I can hang up the key without hurting myself, and without making the hole any bigger. I know I can do almost anything with my fingers. I've often pleased myself when I was a girl with going among mother's bottles in the dark, and getting the one she wanted without upsetting the others.' Susanna again smiled as she looked at those long, tapering, white fingers, with the small rosy nails, blushing at the extremities, and said, 'I know I'm a born lady, that I am. Yes, and if my husband is a gentleman, he shall find I can prove myself as good a lady! Oh, I'll let them see, by-and-by! But I'm forgetting the key.'

Susanna paused, drew back the sleeve of her dress, showing certainly a very beautiful arm, though having the same defect as Susanna's beauty generally—it was too white. But she looked at it herself, almost lovingly, as though she were half inclined to kiss it, as she inserted hand and arm through the broken pane; and then, when she had reached almost as far as she could, she turned the arm a little and felt about for the nail. She grew somewhat nervous at not finding it for a second or two, but at last she touched it, hung on the key, and

drew back her arm without once touching the points
of the glass.

'I'll do it again, to make sure,' thought Susanna;
'who knows how quick I may be obliged to do it,
or how important it may be that I don't give myself
any ugly tell-tale scratches?' And Susanna was
not content till she had drawn the key out, again
put it back, and finally withdrawn her hand, still
with perfect impunity.

'It's good as a play,' laughed Susanna to herself,
as she turned to go back to the cottage.

But as she went through the little gate in the
hedge she saw another 'play' which still more interested her. She saw along the hedge, stretching
a few inches above it, supported by some projecting
twigs, a very fine and beautiful web, just touched
with something that looked like the first hoar frost;
and in a corner, half-concealed by a leaf, a slender
spider of the colour and with the spots that Susanna
so much admired. The creature seemed very
hungry; for nothing, not even a wind-driven twig
or leaf, touched the web but out it flew, retreating
rapidly when aware of its mistake.

'Will she get her breakfast, I wonder, before I get mine?' asked Susanna, and began to take quite new interest in the game before her. Presently a poor half-starved, and entirely chilled bee came heavily floating along, in search, no doubt, of some pleasant flower, out of the calyx of which he might get his breakfast. As luck would have it—or was it more than luck, the special cunning of the lady-spider who sat there under the leaf, feeling so nervously all the threads of her airy trap?—there was a half-decayed flower in the hedge, just under the web, from which came apparently a pleasant and winning scent to the hungry and solitary bee. He hovered about, and Susanna fancied she almost saw the weird little, malignant eyes gazing at him as he did so; and at last he dropped down on the hedge, just outside the web. A pause, a touch, then a great thrill all through the web, but the secret watcher did not run out now. This was a dangerous as well as a precious prey, and must not be inconsiderately meddled with. The bee did not like the feel of the web about his feet, and flew off, to Susanna's great disappointment.

'Cowardly fellow,' thought she, 'to be afraid of a pretty creature like that!' But flowers were scarce, the bee faint and hungry, and he came back, after a few ineffectual circlings and zigzags here and there. Susanna clapped her hands with joy. She wanted to see that contest out. It seemed to her to foreshadow another contest, in which she was personally much interested; and an almost superstitious feeling seemed to say to her,

'If she catches him, so shall I.' The bee touched, and smelt, and touched again, and the spider sprang out and ran back several times; but at last the bee found himself so near to the coveted prize that he began to be less regardful of the tiny web about his feet, which was getting more and more troublesome. Ha! he sees the lyer-in-wait! He springs, or tries to do so: but it is too late; he is caught—wings, legs, body, are enthralled. And now that beautiful monster approaches. He strikes and plunges about convulsively, he wearies himself more and more, she watches him the while, ever drawing nearer as his strength begins to fail; but there is danger in him yet if too hastily assailed. She

knows him well and all his ways. She waits and
watches, and still draws ever more and more nigh,
till the fatal grasp is on him, and then, unable himself to reach the enemy with his sting, he finds her
deadly venom gliding through his veins.

It is wonderful how elated Susanna grew as she
watched the close of this scene. She could have
waited and caught insects herself for that brave and
beautiful spider, but that she had something of the
same kind herself to do ; and besides, as she said to
herself, with a laugh, as she ran to the cottage,

'She's like me, very well able to take care of herself.'

Guy and Stephen had both come down, and were
wondering what had become of Susanna, when she
entered, and cried with her usual pretty air of
surprise,

'Dear me! you *are* up at last! What lie-a-
beds!' Then, as she sat down and began to pour
out the coffee, she observed, 'Somebody or other,
I dare say that Bob, the bird boy, has thrown a
stone and broken a window in the workshop.'

Stephen uttered an angry exclamation ; but

Guy looked moodily in the fire, and seemed to take no notice of his father's complaint.

'Now I shall ha' that to mend! taking up such a deal of time, and so much bother getting a piece of glass all the way from Plackett! I only wish I could lay hands on that youngster, I'd maul him, I warrant!'

'But is it worth mending?' asked Susanna. 'You are never at work there now. The hole may be useful. I can't find one of the keys, so I've hung the other within reach through the broken pane, on the left side, high as you can reach!'

Stephen grumbled something, then said no more on the subject. But presently he turned to Guy and observed,

'What do the squire want o' me?'

'Eh?' asked Guy, starting from his reverie. Stephen repeated the question, adding,

'It was the housekeeper as sent the message, saying the squire would be obligated to me to go to one of his houses and do a little job for him. Them great builders, Noy and Co., of Plackett, allus did his jobs for him afore.'

'Oh, I suppose he thinks he may give you a turn now,' remarked Guy indifferently.

'Well, Mr. Waterman,' said Susanna, 'I think it's a very important matter, and I'd make haste off to see.' Stephen took the advice, to Susanna's great relief, who now found a clear few minutes for a more agreeable chat alone with Guy. She determined to lose no time, so began the very instant Stephen left the room.

'Well, Guy dear, I'm going to stay for a few days with my guardian.'

'Your guardian!' echoed Guy, in surprise, 'Oh, I know. Mr. Gage!' He said this with such supreme coolness that Susanna felt stung.

'Well, he is my guardian, isn't he? and he's getting a very respectable man—he's had a deal of money left him, and given up carrying, and bought himself such a beautiful horse and chaise.'

'Yes,' said Guy, waiting for Susanna to proceed, and explain about her new movement in relation to her 'guardian.'

'Well, dear, I've been talking to him about my position here, and he quite agrees that it isn't a fit

thing for a young lady to stay in the same house
with her affianced lover, now that there's no mother
alive.'

'Well?' asked Guy.

'Well, dear, I shall go to-day. My only ob-
jection is that your poor father won't be made so
comfortable as I could wish. He needs his home
and comforts. He's got used to it, you know.
And what sort of home can *she* make for him?'
Susanna here pointed to the dirty, little, miserable,
red-eyed girl who was going past the window carrying a pan of coals.

'I'm sorry, Susanna, you have had all this trouble
for nothing. I ought to have told you, but I forgot,
that I shall stay at the Hall for the present, so you
and father needn't make any change.'

'At the Hall,' thought Susanna; 'what does
that mean? I think I know; but I'll make sure.
Yes, that I will!' So, after a pause, she said,
looking sidelong at Guy the while,

'Miss Lucy coming home soon?' Guy started,
the colour came into his cheeks, he seemed almost
to tremble with passion. The sidelong look winced

just a little under his fierce gaze—but only a little, and did not turn away. Guy pushed his hand through his hair, walked across the floor, and then said, in a deep, thrilling voice,

'Susanna, if you value our engagement; if—if you really wish to marry me you will take care that this is the last time you mention the name of Miss Dalrymple as you have now mentioned it.'

'Why, Guy, dear,' exclaimed Susanna—and Guy could not but see the tears gathering in the soft blue eyes, and the look of tender reproach overshadowing the whole of the fair face, as she spoke, 'Why, Guy dear, what did you suppose I meant? I only asked because I thought she might be returning, and be—be—be-cause' (Susanna was now sobbing) 'I thought while you were thinking about so many things else you had quite forgotten her—her return I mean—which I am sure you would not like to take place while you are there, and—while—' But here Susanna's voice melted away into utter indistinctness.

'No, Susanna, you are right in that. Good-by.' Guy took his hat, and without another word, or even his usual kiss at parting, went away, while she watched through the window his retreating form, and seemed to say, as the lady-spider had apparently said,

'Never mind. He'll come back.'

CHAPTER VIII.

THE SQUIRE'S PLOT.

CERTAINLY, Susanna's star was this day in the ascendant, notwithstanding the untoward-looking sky. Guy had not been many hours gone, when she saw a vehicle that she knew belonged to the squire, for it was the same that had taken her and Phœbe and Guy to the court during Pample's trial, come rapidly through the village towards the house and stop right opposite the door. She ran out, and the man said,

'If you please, Miss, Mrs. Hammett says the squire wishes you to go with me for a short ride to-day.'

'Oh, certainly, certainly;' said Susanna, colouring, for once, with natural pleasure. 'Wait, I won't be long.' She hurried off to her bed-room, and ransacked her boxes right and left, to find a sufficiently handsome and distinguished-looking silk dress, saying to herself,

'I wonder whether I shall see the squire? I have heard that your grand ladies don't like to appear twice in the same dress. I wonder which of these dresses he has before seen me in at church? I can't at all remember. Dear me, what can it all be about? How very sudden!'

Susanna dressed fast, the woman's vanity in her being always more or less kept under control by the conspirator's instinct of caution as to her interests; she did not know what she might lose if she were too long dressing; so she soon came back to the man outside, and gave him one of her very sweetest smiles as he stood with the door open, and then she got in and was driven rapidly off.

'How nice,' thought Susanna, 'to be always driving about in a carriage like this, and with a servant like that! What will he say, I wonder, one day when he finds I am the lady of Branhape, and his mistress?'

We will not follow Susanna at present on her mysterious journey, but see what the squire is thinking of when he meets Guy, after making such incomprehensible arrangements.

Guy found him in a chair, being wheeled about in the kitchen-garden by a servant. The walks there were straight and broad, and more convenient for such exercise than the winding paths of the beautiful pleasure-grounds: they were also more sunny. As Guy approached, the squire called out good-humouredly,

'Here I am, laid up again with this confounded gout. But I won't give way. I have had this old chair exhumed from its long resting-place. I can get air and the blessed sun, at all events, in spite of the gout. Ah!' Here his face changed, and could not be prevented from showing to Guy the sudden and intense pain he felt. 'Oh, don't mind; it'll go soon. There, it's better already. I'll have a boot on again within a week and take another run with the hounds. George,' said he, to the man-servant, 'push me indoors now, and then tell them to get the chariot out.' As they went along, Guy keeping at his side, his face reflecting every pang he saw in the squire's countenance, the

latter said, ' I think, now you've come, we'll have a
quiet drive together; I want to talk to you about
two or three matters.'

In a few minutes they were driving along
through the park. Mr. Dalrymple seemed to
borrow new life from the crispness of the autumnal
air, the warmth of the sun, and the rich hues of the
foliage. He talked incessantly; told the story of
every great tree they came across; raised up in
Guy's mind image after image of the persons
among whom Mr. Dalrymple had spent his early
life, most of them, as Guy believed, his own blood
relatives; and at last glanced at a theme that
possessed even still deeper interest for him — Lucy.

' Yes; I want her back. I want her back now,'
said the squire, and Guy thought there was a
something in the tone that was meant for him.

' Does he change his views regarding me?' was
the first half insane idea that leaped into existence
in Guy's brain. 'Is he going to say something
that—fool! fool! be still. Let no one—he, least
of all—see your folly.' The squire soon settled
his notion.

'Of course your purpose holds as regards the marriage with Susanna?'

'Yes,' faltered out Guy; for what else could he say? If some sort of blind instinct had been lately whispering to him, 'Pause, wait; this new discovery may, in some mode unsuspected by you, yet change your fate, yet relieve you of your promise' —he had still been obliged, as a man of honour, to refuse to listen to it; ay, even when it went further, and suggested, 'Would *he* allow it if he knew? Ought you not to submit the matter to him?'—Guy still felt bound to answer, 'Too late! Too late! I have promised, distinctly promised, and can only break that promise by becoming a rascal. She loves me; loves me at least as well as she can love anybody or thing other than herself; she is virtuous; and has done nothing to justify me in saying she is unworthy to be my wife.'

All this passed as with lightning's speed through Guy's mind while he hesitated just for a single moment to answer the squire's question, before pronouncing the word that just now seemed to have a fateful sound—the little word 'Yes.'

The squire dropped the subject and again began to talk of his early days, as though there was something in Guy's presence or behaviour that brought them back to him. Guy, on his part, was beginning to understand in what direction they were going.

'Surely,' thought he, 'we are going to the steward's house. What for, I wonder? Is he going to put *me* there?' What else he thought we need not dwell on, for the carriage soon stopped before one of those quaint mediæval-looking houses which are the delight of the antiquary, and of the student of the picturesque. It was only a two-storied house, was flat, had no gables, and yet was unmistakably ancient. The windows were all of stone, and mullioned; the front roof-line curved in a peculiarly fanciful way in the centre into ornament; a pomegranate-tree covered nearly every inch of the surface; and a shield of arms, showing faint traces of colour, occupied the centre, just below the ornamental curve of the roof. The building looked out on a little garden which might have been supposed to have been only recently walled off from the heathy, ferny sward on which the whole stood, on a natural rise of the soil, were it not that the low stone hedge was covered with green moss and lichens; and that the box and evergreen plants, and the antique sundial in it, had evidently been undisturbed for generations. Not far off was a little stream that came trickling and winding down from the neighbouring hill, and forming, high up, quite a waterfall. Guy knew the place well, though he had not often had occasion to see it.

'Pretty place!' said the squire.

'Very,' said Guy, looking round with deep admiration.

'And yet I fancy that poor unhappy man Pample never cared for it He used to be, as you know, almost always at the Hall after I had once invited him to stay with me a few days. Help me down and let us go in.'

They went in, and Guy found the inside even more to his taste than the exterior. There were such pleasant nooks and corners all about it, and there was so much fine old carving, of which Guy was especially fond, as having himself skill in that art, that he was perfectly delighted. They went upstairs, in spite of the gout, for the squire insisted on showing Guy the whole place. Presently they came to a little room that might have been originally designed either as a lady's boudoir, if she cared more for nature than for art, or for a poet's study, if, indeed, a poet could have written with sufficient self-concentration in sight of the lovely little landscape seen through the window which opened to the ground and had a wooden balcony outside. You saw nothing from that window but the hillside, the waterfall, the woods at the sides of black pine and graceful silvery birch, and the sky above; but that eye must indeed have been exacting that sought for more.

The squire's eyes moistened as he sat by the window, while Guy went out and stood upon the balcony, leaning against the wall, so that he could hear if the squire spoke to him. And he did hear presently something that he would never again fail to associate with this beautiful place.

'It was here, Guy, that I and my wife settled

that very serious business of matrimony. And what a day it was! I don't think it was because of my feeling just then that I thought it without exception the most truly perfect day I had ever seen. She thought the same. This house was not then given up to the steward. It was reserved—as it had been built—for some member of the family who might like to be near the Hall without being obliged to live in it. It was empty, and we came to spend an hour or two, and before we went out it was all settled. You know her picture in my study, Guy. But it does not do her justice. I think she was the most beautiful woman, in the more spiritual sense of the word beauty, that I ever saw; and not only the most beautiful, but the sweetest by nature—the tenderest in her affections. Some priest got between us and spoiled our lives for us. But Guy, I loved her dearly; I love her still; and, there!—you've heard me more garrulous than I think I ever was in my life before on such matters. Growing very old, I suppose.' He sighed and was silent.

Ah! if he could have known how he had filled

to overflowing the whole heart and soul of the
listener by his talk! If he could but have known
that there by his side was her son and his,—a youth
worthy of all the love and pride he could ever
desire to feel, but condemned by cruel circumstances to veil his emotions and listen as he listens
now, breathlessly, but with the outward air of one
who listens to a superior, and to matters on which
he has no right to comment in return.

The prolonged silence was broken by the sound
of a hammer. The squire smiled, and said to Guy,

'See who that is, and bring him here.'

Guy ran into an adjoining room, and as he
had begun to anticipate, found Stephen at work
arranging the blinds and window - curtains, and
standing on the top of some tall steps. He stared
at Guy, who laughed at his surprise and said,

'You must come in; the squire wants you.'

'Wants me?' Stephen came slowly down, re-
volving by the way the question of the squire's
probable wants, which might be very profitable to
Stephen if the squire really did mean to employ
him. They returned together to the squire, who

shook hands with Stephen, the latter looking doubtfully at his own hard, horny, and not very clean
palms before venturing to submit to such an honour.

'Well, Mr. Waterman, I want now to have the
place made thoroughly comfortable.   Everything
put to rights.   Can you manage it, think you?'

'I'll try, sir, said Stephen.

'Very good.   Do everything effectually; don't
let us have any afterclaps.   Sound roof, sound windows, sound drainage—they're half the battle.   By-
the-by, I wish we had the help of a lady to tell us
what is requisite in other matters.   The furniture
wants a good deal of overhauling, I suspect.   Hark!
There's a carriage!   Guy, run and see who it is.
How very lucky if it should be some female friend
or other!'   The squire looked archly at Stephen,
who stared at him and then looked after Guy and
began secretly to wonder if anything was going
wrong with the squire's upper works.   Anyhow,
Stephen couldn't at all make him out to-day.

When Guy got to the front-door he found, to
his astonishment, Susanna just descending from the
carriage.

'What's all this about?' he asked bluntly.

'I'm sure I don't know, Guy dear. The man came to fetch me, and brought me here. What a pretty place! Oh, what a heavenly place to live in. Well, I never did see so sweet a place in all my life!'

Guy was confounded—no longer, however, by his ignorance, but by his knowledge. He saw and with an intense feeling of dislike, and with a great desire to shrink back out of the too-fervent sunshine of the squire's favour, that the visit to-day of all parties to this place was a planned thing: a little plot of the squire's own, suggested by his kindness of heart, and perhaps also by his secret determination to hurry on Guy's marriage in order that Lucy might come back. He took Susanna's outstretched hand, and led her in silence up the stairs, taking no notice of her running comment of admiration of everything she saw.

'Good-day, young lady,' said the squire, rising to his full height and taking off his hat with courtly grace, then stretching out his hand to hers, which he took and clasped warmly in his large palm, 'I

am much obliged by your prompt consent to favour
me with your presence here. I want your advice a
bit. I want to see this favourite old place of mine
refreshed and made habitable. I want the Pample
stain taken out of it. It is a house very dear to
me. Let's have it purified first, then made pleasant.
There's some good old furniture which I rather
lean to. Keep that; but burn the rubbish, and
give Mrs. Hammett or me a list of deficiencies.
Come, now; suppose — I only say for a moment
suppose—that some friend of yours was going to
be married in it. Ah, Guy! I see young ladies
haven't forgotten how to blush; nor, I suppose, have
they become less conscious how pretty it makes
them. There, Guy, you rogue! take her away,
and settle all the rest yourselves, and leave the two
elders to potter a bit longer over things too mun-
dane for your attention.'

What could Guy do, but as he was bidden?
Fate had willed it: he must renounce even his last
dream of the possibility of relief from this marriage.
Well, he would do it; ay, as heroically as the
martyr goes to the stake. It was, indeed, a very

martyr-like smile he turned on Susanna as he muttered something to her, and they went out to take together that communion about their future which was to be so different from what his father and mother had known in the same place.

'Oh! Guy, dear,' said Susanna, 'how very sudden! I assure you I hadn't the least idea of what I was coming for.'

'Nor I, I assure you;' and again Guy smiled. 'Well, luckily, he has spared us the necessity of much talk. He has settled everything for us, it seems. Here is to be our home, and we shan't even have the perplexity of furnishing.'

'Yes; it's very good of the squire, now, isn't it?'

'Oh, very!'

'But did you say he had settled everything, Guy, dear?' asked Susanna, in tones of touching tenderness.

'Yes, I think so. What else?'

'The—the—day!'

'The day? True, I forgot that. Shall we ask him?' Was there something too bitterly ironical in the tone even for Susanna to put up with?

She suddenly stopped, burst into tears, and ex-claimed,

'You don't want me, I do believe!'

'Now, Susanna, don't be childish!'

'No; you don't want me. I shall go home—yes, I will,' and she turned, evidently bent on going back with the carriage, thus making public to the squire the true state of Guy's relations with her. The idea maddened him. Lucy! That would be the squire's first thought. It was for Lucy. Guy ran after her, seized her arm, drew her to a more secluded part of the grounds (and still farther away from the house), and said,

'Susanna, I warn you, if you actually refuse to marry me now, and humiliate me before the squire, as you will by so doing, I will receive such refusal as final, and abide by it afterwards, no matter at what cost. On the other hand, if—if I have not seemed—well, I may say, have not been what I ought to be—to one in your position, which I have not, I acknowledge that honestly, I still say you know the reason; and you may, if you will, sympa-thize with me, and then—well, then all will remain as it was, and I will do my best to make you a good husband, and love you as you deserve for your long love to me.   Now choose ; but don't do it in sudden pique or jealousy. Choose like a sensible, honest woman.'

'Oh Guy ! dear, dear, dear Guy !' And Susanna fell weeping on his neck ; and he embraced her, and swore with true emotion, she should not, if he could help it, repent of this her final choice.

While he then looked round upon the place, the house, the waterfall, and thought it would be hard if he could not enjoy life there with such a companion to give it new beauty, he drew in something like peace.   And how was she engaged?   Why, she was already looking back, thinking with a smile of that poor bee and the lady-spider, and looking forward to the far greater triumphs that yet awaited her, and which made even this lovely spot contemptible in her eyes, if she had told the truth, when she compared it with the lordly splendour of Branhape.

'Just a month, then, this day,' whispered Guy.

'It's very little,' murmured Susanna, in answer,

'but just as you please, darling. I have only now
evermore to think how I may best please you.'

And so they went back to the squire, who looked
radiant with the success of his plot; and to Stephen,
who grew quite scared in his joy at the idea that he
was to live in this place with Guy and his bride, and
should not need to work any more, except to keep
his hand in and to please his own fancies.

'Well, Guy,' said the squire, a few minutes
later, when Susanna had gone off with Stephen, full
of her new duties, 'I don't regret even now of that
which was done here, though things didn't end so
happily as I could have wished. I hope you'll live
to give even a better report of your day's work to
somebody else when I'm gone.'

And then he became silent, and the eyes moistened once more, and he sat there a long time,
while Guy kept near, feeling as if his heart were
beating in unison with every motion of the squire's.

CHAPTER IX.

GUY'S WEDDING DAY.

SUSANNA was now in her glory. The assured certainty of success, while it did not relax in the slightest her instinct of caution, gave new vigour to her mind, new elasticity to her frame, new softness to her eye, new splendour to her beauty. She grew also more winning in manner, and one might almost have fancied, more humble in soul, but for a certain impatience that would now and then break out and make a jar in the prevailing harmony of things; but this happened only before unimportant persons, with whom, perhaps, she thought it necessary to play the 'lady;' never to Guy, or to the squire, or even to Stephen. Susanna had in her Scripture reading, while acting as a teacher in the Sunday school, managed to preserve in memory one text as particularly valuable, and altogether suited to her position and views, and that was, the being all things to all men. Just now Susanna grew quite religious, if the fullest possible study and exemplification of the Apostle's injunction could make her so.

Her life also had now its one period of romance. The ceaseless rummaging about the fine old house which the squire had placed at her and Guy's disposal; the ordering about of a crowd of workmen and upholsterers; the going into Plackett with Guy in the squire's carriage to purchase curtains for the windows, hangings for the bed, and carpets for the floor; the shopping in the streets of Plackett, partly with Guy, partly without him, while he went to settle business matters with the squire's solicitors; the ravishing display of silks, and satins, and ribbons laid out before her at the chief draper's; and then, the going to the jeweller's to buy bracelets, and a diamond neck-pin for Guy, while he, in return, not only selected a handsome gold watch to give to her, but did what, perhaps, Susanna had secretly supposed he might do on such an occasion —made her try on a pretty ring, which did not fit

her, and which therefore he did not buy, as though
to know the measure for a different kind of ring;—
this kind of life was delicious to Susanna, nor did
she trouble herself by asking how far her feelings
were shared by her companion.

Still there were occasional vexations. One day,
while she was standing in what was to be their
future drawing-room, admiring the pattern of the
new carpet that had been purchased and brought
home, and which had been rolled out before her by
the man who was to fit it, she saw Guy, who had
come at her request to judge of the effect, reading a
piece of paper, which seemed to startle him very
much. How he had obtained it Susanna could not
perceive, for she had not noticed anyone speak to
him. He read and read again, then turned, and
handed the paper to her, and waited while she read
it, with eyes fixed full upon her. This was the
letter :—

*'Mind what you are about, I ain't at liberty to
speak plain, nor do I know enough most likely to con-
vince you if I tried. But I say again, mind what*

*you are about. I've long had my doubts of secret
motives at work. I feel sure on it now. If you can't
make up your mind to stop afore it's too late, then I
advise you to put off as long as possible.*

'A FRIEND.'

"Who could have written it?' asked Susanna,
when she had read the whole.

'I havn't the least idea in the world.'

'It is a very strange kind of writing,' remarked
Susanna.

'Yes; it looks to me like what I should imagine
a man or a woman might do if they wrote for the
first time with the left hand.'

'To disguise the real hand?' she inquired.

'Yes.'

Susanna began to turn the letter about, in order
to glance at it in all sorts of positions—to hold it
up to the light, that she might look through it;
but she seemed baffled in all her endeavours to
make even a guess at the writer. Guy grew impatient.

'Why don't you try to find out the meaning of

the letter, instead of hunting after the writer of
it ?'

'Why, Guy dear, for this reason ;—I might guess
at the one, but I can't, you know, at the other.
How could I ?'

With an air of disappointment Guy merely said,
'You can't?'

'No,' Susanna replied firmly ; 'but, don't you
see, Guy dear, if we only find out the writer we
might then find out his meaning.'

'That's true.' So they began to speculate on all
the possibilities or probabilities. Susanna had but
one suggestion to offer — 'Mrs. Hammett;' but
Guy so laughed at the idea, and altogether treated
it so disrespectfully, that Susanna bridled, and left
him to guess for himself. And then they ceased
any longer to discuss the incident.

Guy wondered whether he should hear again
before the marriage-day from his anonymous correspondent. But Friday dawned at last—the day
fixed for the wedding, and still the unknown made
no sign. Guy rose and began to dress. He was

still at the Hall, and Susanna still at the cottage; and the plan was that they should go from the church to 'The Knoll,' and there Mrs. Hammett would receive them and give up possession to the future inmates. The morning was bright, though icy cold; and the ground was everywhere white with the pure untrodden snow that had fallen during the last few hours. On one side the pine and other forest trees around looked spectral in their snowy drapery; while on the other, where the sun shone through them, Guy saw the most exquisite tints of purple and gold, that seemed to belong to a different order of life, and to say to him, 'Whatever of sorrow or discontent you may know in your earthly lot, here, at least, is heaven—the heaven that you and your fellows will only dream of—not work for.'

Guy rapidly completed the process of dressing. His wedding suit was a very plain one. He looked pale and haggard, but there was that indefinable air about him which stamps the real as contrasted with the artificial gentleman. There was refinement, in spite of occasional awkwardness; there was personal dignity, but unaccompanied by any of that self-assertion which seems only to find due gratification when it can make the dignity of other and especially of poorer men bend before it; there was a thoughtful yet soft eye; a powerful yet winning and modulated voice; a tall and athletic body, that seemed to have been moulded throughout by a gentle spirit working ceaselessly and unconsciously from within. Such was Guy as the squire met him that morning in the park, and looked at him with even more than his usual kindliness of feeling.

But what is the squire doing on horseback on a day like this, and at his time of life, and after so many recent hints from his doctor about the ' rascally gout?' Why, he himself tells Guy, as if to anticipate any remonstrances—

'Well, Guy, lad, you're off, I see, and all happiness go with you. I shall look in upon you in the evening; but meantime, you see I'm off too. There now, my good, kind lad, I don't want any remonstrances. I mean to be careful. But come, I'll tell you a secret. It won't hurt you now. Lucy comes back to-morrow, I hope; and I know the peremptory little tyrant will stop all this kind of thing when she does come. So I'm taking time by the forelock. What a glorious morning! The hounds meet at the "Furze Bushes." Good-by! Wish me a good run, for it will be my last!'

And the squire, putting spurs to his horse, galloped off, leaving Guy standing there, and saying to himself, in mournful despair.

'Oh, if he but knew! If he but knew! But he does not, and I cannot tell him till I can defy all dispute or contradiction. No. God bless him! May he, as he wishes, have a pleasant ride to-day! So he has written already to Lucy, has he? I wonder what he said, and whether he mentioned me?'

As Guy goes along towards the cottage where his bride awaits him, suppose, by the aid of that more than mesmeric power which writers of fiction possess, or assume to possess, we look into the letter that Lucy has just received, and is now reading, precisely at the time that Guy is going off to meet his bride :—

'My Darling Lucy,—I really can extend your reprieve no longer. The blow that has been so long overhanging you—threatening to take you once more from your home, your parents, your young companions, and the amusements natural to your age, must fall ; and even if you acknowledge you wince at it, you must submit, must come back to your poor old despotic uncle, who now begs you to return to him without delay. But, in sober earnest, I do, my darling girl, want you back. I have been reckoning up, day by day, the number of days that must still pass before I can see your sweet, glad, though most hypocritical face, for it always manages to look pleasant at me, no matter how bad my temper or unreasonable my demands. But there is nothing now to wait for—*nothing*—so come.

' Let me see ; is there any particular news to tell you? Guy will be married to-morrow morning about the time this letter will reach you, and immediately afterwards will be comfortably settled with his wife at " The Knoll." I have given them, you see, the steward's house, which has been thoroughly renovated, and is now, indeed, a cosy, delightful old place. I shall not say much on this subject, nor do I think you wish me, or need it ;

but my heart is with you. This, however, I should like to say: Now that there is no longer a question of his being more to you than a friend, you will, I hope, *in due time*, when you can reflect on the past with perfect quietude, I say you will then, I hope, treat him *as* a friend. I like him better the more I see of him. And that, between ourselves, is more than I can say of his wife. I was going to tell you of sundry other interesting home facts, but on second thoughts I shall do nothing of the kind, not at least till I see you here, and know you are duly obedient.

'So, the day after to-morrow, at five o'clock, you will find the carriage at the old place, waiting for the coach that brings you back to the arms of your old and, I suspect, doting uncle,

'GODFREY DALRYMPLE.

'P.S.—Shall I tell you what I am just going to do? Ha! ha! young lady! I am going, then, to have my last run with the hounds. My horse is at the door. I have got on my boot with a few twinges, I confess, but still it is on! But mind, this is positively the last time! Lucy, I say it on the honour of a gentleman, positively the last time. I needn't tell you, I suppose, *why* I take this opportunity *before you come back.* Eh, you saucy, tyrannical little puss?

'2nd P.S.—I find that the coach which used to reach our meeting-place at 5 does not now get there till near midnight. Is it, darling, too much to ask you to set out, then, to-morrow, so that you may sleep at the inn at night, and be ready when I send for you the next morning early, say at 10 o'clock? Arrangements have been made for your comfort at the inn.   G. D.'

Such was the squire's letter.

. . . . ; . . .

The church and the churchyard are thronged with people, for Guy has become famous since the great trial, and everybody wants to see if it be actually true that he is going to marry—not the young lady who confessed in public her love for him, but another lady, said to be even more beautiful than Miss Dalrymple. They wait impatiently, for they begin to think the bridal party late. Still there is delay, and rumours begin to circulate that something has happened. It is even whispered that the squire has had a bad fall, and that Guy must have gone back to the Hall with him. But carriage wheels are heard. Yes; the party comes at last, in three vehicles, which bring the few nearest friends who had been assembled at the cottage — the others are already in the church. Mr. Gage gets out, puffing and blowing at the exertion; Susanna's 'guardian' is to give her away. From the last carriage Guy jumps to the ground, and hands forth two showily-dressed bridesmaids, who, it must be acknowledged, are not pretty; Susanna has taken care of that.

But as the party enter the church and pass along the aisle, Guy hears some one drop the words 'squire' and 'accident.' He looks; it is Joshua Darkley, attired in his best, who is speaking to a neighbour. Guy stops, just as he is, with one of the ladies on his arm, and says with suppressed emotion

'Did you say an accident had happened to the squire?'

'Well, they says so. I'm told he fell in leaping over a ditch, and is badly hurt, though not so bad but he may get over it.'

'Susanna, did you hear?' Guy asked, going towards her, for she, too, had stopped in wonder and secret alarm.

'Yes, Guy dear ; but you know we can't help it just now. See, the minister is waiting for us. Suppose you run over to the Hall the moment you leave the church.'

Guy looked at her, and Susanna smiled her old and fascinating smile, but it had no longer the remotest fascination for him. He said, after a pause,

'Yes, yes, I must do that.' Then, after another pause, and while they resumed positions, he added in a tone that seemed to be meant for gaiety, but was, in fact, anything rather than that, and which was addressed to the plain young lady on his arm,

'Is not my wife beautiful?' The poor girl, knowing her own want of beauty, coloured at the inconsiderateness of the remark, but said,

'She is indeed ! You ought to be very happy.'

'Happy ! I'm the most blissful dog alive. But, take my advice, when you marry, trouble only yourself with one question—what will your husband think of you a month after marriage ? ' The young lady seemed to understand that this was a sort of hint as to her *goodness*, intended to carry off the unlucky remark about Susanna's *beauty*; and although she would have preferred the other state of things, she smiled graciously and seemed contented with the one which Guy assigned her.

A few minutes more, and Guy saluted Susanna as his lawful wedded wife; the woman whom he had sworn to love and cherish; and whom, whatever she might be, he was bound to take with all her faults, and make the best of.

.   .   .   .

The twilight is just melting into the early winter evening. Sounds of merriment issue from the brilliantly-lighted windows. Dancing is going on vigorously. Susanna has no notion of slurring over so great an occasion. Other brides may steal away into privacy as soon as they can, she will not. This is for her a day of immeasurable triumph. None yet know but herself how great a triumph! To reach this pinnacle she has schemed and disciplined her whole nature into habitual deception; and has felt naturally the whole time a sense of weight, of

responsibility, arising from the fear of failure. But
all that is over. She is cheerful, light-hearted at
last. Is she not Guy's wife? What that means she
waits only a few days to reveal to the world.

How magnificent she looks in her pure white
gossamer robe, with the broad silver stripes running
up and down! As she goes smiling and gliding,
twisting and turning in the dance, she looks won-
drously like a splendid white woman-snake—all
glitter and shine and softness—while her pale blue
eyes and fair hair give her at the same time an angelic expression. Her shoulders are perfectly
dazzling. And though she seems to look and look
towards the door for Guy's return from the Hall,
she still dances on as if incapable of fatigue ;
and as the others grow hot and red, she appears to
grow colder and whiter, and more light of foot every
minute.

Guy comes at last. He looks pale as death, and
he speaks so low that the young lady addressed can
only just catch the meaning of his words. He has
asked, looking towards Susanna as if he wanted her,

‘ Has the dance just begun ? ’

' No, it will soon be over,' was the reply.

So Guy waited and watched the passage to and fro of the silvery snaky stripes and the angelic head till the dancers stopped, the music ceased, and she came towards him.

' Well, Guy dear, how is he?'

' I doubt if he will live through the night.'

Susanna stared at him a moment incredulously, then her whole manner changed. She became excited, fidgety, restless, though her words did not seem to reflect or be in harmony with the expression of her face and gestures.

' Then you'll go back to the Hall? Don't mind me. Very sad—our wedding night, isn't it? But don't mind me.'

' Well, Susanna, I think I ought to go there, as you say.'

' Yes, yes. Go, dear Guy. Go at once. I will speak to them and excuse you.'

And Susanna hurried him off. But it so happened that Guy stopped for a few minutes downstairs to speak to one of the guests about additional medical aid, and thus some time was lost. But he got himself free, and while putting on his cloak in the hall to face the winter eve, and while listening with indescribable anguish to the merry mockeries of the music and the dance, he felt his hand touched. He looked round. There were several persons passing, but no one that he could fix on as having touched him. Then he saw at his feet a bit of paper. He took it up, and read by the light of the hall lamp these words :—

' *Maybe you'll mind me now, and wish when it's too late you'd a minded me afore, when I tells you to look for your—— If you're a bit surprised, as'll very likely happen, you'll maybe listen this time to a* friend, *who says—Go as fast as you can go to the workshop at Tanfield. Get there first, and don't let anybody see you a-going.*'

Guy's first impulse on reading the note was to run out into the open air, and look round in the bright moonlight for Susanna. But, seeing nothing of her he returned hurriedly to the house, and meeting one of the bridemaids, who had just de-

scended the stairs from the dance, said, vainly trying to quell the agitation of his tones, 'Is my wife
still in the drawing-room?'

'No; she went out some minutes ago, saying she
felt so fatigued and shocked by the news from the
Hall, that she thought she should go to her room,
and leave the company for the night.'

'Thank you,' said Guy, as he ran up the stairs,
glanced in at the dancers, then went to the bed-
chamber, tapped at the door, found, as he expected,
no reply; tried the door, but it was locked; so he
put his shoulder against it, and exerting his whole
strength, burst it in. The room was empty. He
looked everywhere about. He opened a closet
door; that place too was empty. He left the room
after managing to so dispose of the door and its
broken lock as to conceal his violence from any
casual observer, and ran from room to room to
examine every part of the house before he would
finally accept the plain fact that Susanna had
slipped away directly she thought he had gone.
Once convinced of that, he said to himself, 'So the
writer of this knows what he talks about! She *has*

gone out, from such a scene, and at such a time, and given an untrue reason for doing so. Very well; look to yourself, now, Susanna.'

Guy was soon once more outside the house, crushing down the snow with rapid steps. At first he began merely to walk as fast as he could, because he was within sight from the windows; but when they and their lights disappeared from his view through the descent of the heathy snow-covered surface, and through the interposition of clumps of low-growing trees, he began to run swiftly.

The moon was rising in front, and every projecting object that intercepted its light stood out dark and impressive. Yet he nowhere saw a single trace of Susanna. On he ran, keeping the while a most zealous watch that he might not come suddenly upon her, and so be seen. He wanted now to know exactly what she knew; to see, without possibility of being deceived by her artifices, what it was that she was plotting to carry into effect. He was most anxious, therefore, not to interrupt her, or to raise any kind of fear in her mind that she was being watched. He was obliged, in consequence, to adopt a very devious route, making from one place of shelter to another—a tree-trunk, a hedge, or a depression in the soil—tacking about at all sorts of angles, like a ship contending with difficult winds. The worst of this was, it took up so much time that he began to fear that he would not overtake Susanna at all.

Where can she be? He ascends now a little mound that gives him command over a long stretch of white country, glittering in the beautiful light. Still no Susanna. What can it mean? He suddenly remembers that there is an old and generally dried-up water-course or small river-bed that runs right across the heath, with high, sloping banks, where she may, if she knows the spot well, glide along a footpath at a low level without a chance of being observed from the ordinary routes across the heath. Guy strikes off towards it, when, happening to look back, he sees something like a human form moving towards him. He stands still. The figure does the same, and Guy fancies it to be a small tree to which his excited vision alone has given humanity. He moves towards it, and it disappears, as if swallowed up by the ground.

'Was that Susanna?' he asks; but he thinks not, and hurries on—a little too fast considering the inequalities of the ground, and the treacherous character of the comparatively even surface made by the snow, for he suddenly pitched head forwards many feet down a declivity, rolling among the snow, while he tried with desperate hands to grasp in passing some of the low bushes. Bruised and shaken, with his mouth and hands full of the snow, he quickly regained his feet; and trying to take no notice of his fall, gazed earnestly first to the right, then to the left, for he was aware he was at the exact spot he had wished to reach, though he had miscalculated the distance in reaching it so suddenly and unpleasantly. Still no Susanna. Guy now, turning a little to the right, climbed up the bank again in a diagonal direction, by the aid of the bushes, out of which he had so effectually shaken the snow; and, keeping his body close to the ground, made way to a rock that he happened to remember as overhanging the edge of the little hill, and as forming below a kind of recess which he as a boy had helped other boys to enlarge almost into a cave by digging away the soft sand. He had scarcely reached this place of cover when he heard, as he had expected he should hear, slow muffled steps approaching, but with greater care than he himself had used. Then, after a brief pause, Guy saw a head—only a head, no more—just advance from the snowy line of the bank, and pause there thus projected, evidently on the look-out. For some time it remained almost motionless, and Guy tried to make out how it was covered, whether by a woman's close-fitting hood or a man's cap—for it was certainly one or the other—but he could not, for the part lay in shadow.

After a prolonged pause the head was drawn back; but Guy did not move; and presently he saw the entire form re-emerge, descending the bank. Would it go straight down, or come towards Guy along the path that had been worn by the boy-visitors to the cave? The form chose the latter, either because the descent that way was safer, or to get the benefit of the rock while trying to evade observation, and so it passed out of Guy's sight, even while he heard it come nearer and nearer, crunching the snow at every step. He hears the hard breathing; he sees the dark shadow quite close. It is that of a man, obviously. Guy resolved in an instant what to do. As the figure went past where he lay and began to burrow close to the snow in order to get lower down and over a more exposed position, Guy rose stealthily to his feet by the aid of his hands against the rock, and suddenly precipitated himself with his whole weight upon the stranger, who fell in an agony of alarm upon the snow, making no outcry, but breathing heavily, while Guy, on his part, grappled the man by the throat where he lay, and murmured in deep, suppressed tones,

'Be quiet, as you value your life!'

Again the man breathed heavily, and Guy tried to make out his face, as he said to him in the same low tone (for he feared alarming Susanna, who might be near),

'Speak! who are you? Why, is it possible? Joshua Darkley! In Heaven's name, what does all this mean?'

'Take your hands off my throat, and I may have a chance to tell you,' was Joshua's reply, made in a tone of intense anger or vexation.

'Friend or foe? Tell me that honestly—like a man,' said Guy, relaxing but not altogether quitting his grasp.

'You don't give a man a fair chance of answering sich a question, when you lies in wait for him, and throttles him.'

'Upon my soul, Joshua, I beg your pardon a thousand times if I have done you wrong. I scarcely know what I am about. But again I ask, are you here as a friend?'

'Well, I s'pose I may say—yes.'

Give me a proof, and you shall find me grateful.'

'You are *going to the workshop*, ain't you?'

Guy put out his hand in silence. Joshua took it, and there was a strong and cordial grasp exchanged. Guy knew now his secret correspondent. For a minute not a word more was spoken. Then Guy broke out with,

'I cannot find her. Has she gone this way, think you?'

'I've no doubt she's a-going this way; and I don't think she's passed.'

'If not, what had best be done?'

'Wait under the rock till we see her go by.'

'But the note told me to get to the workshop first—.'

'And so you can. Soon as you sees her a-going in the direction we expects, you'll be sure I have rightly guessed what she's after; and then you may leave her to find her own road, while you run to the workshop by the nearest way.'

'Very well.' And then the two cautiously drew within the deep shade of the rock, to wait.

'Joshua,' said Guy, a little later, and after some cogitation with himself, 'this is a strange business, and possibly a wretchedly false position for us all. You could have had no motive in writing but to serve me. Will you now say plainly what it was you referred to when you spoke of 'motives' in connection with Susanna—I mean with my wife; for I suppose you intended me to apply your warning to her?'

Joshua coughed, and made no other answer.

But Guy understood, and repeated his question with increased earnestness.

'I'd rather you'd guess for yourself,' was the sexton's cautious reply. Guy was growing angry and impatient. He could not understand this cowardly kind of friendship. But he had the good sense to remember that he must take Joshua as he was, and be only the more ready to acknowledge that the sexton was, for so prudent a man, really doing a great deal for the benefit of another. But he could not go on playing a child's game. He must be sure that his own thought was also Joshua's; so he began :—

'Whatever I may now fancy—however wild or improbable my thoughts may be—remember it is you who are answerable for them—'

'I answerable!' interposed the sexton. 'I objects to that statement.'

'Confound you, Joshua, what do you mean? Of course, I don't mean responsible in anything injurious to yourself. Look you. If your letter had any meaning at all, it meant one of two things—to make some charge against my wife's personal character—'

'I never dreamed o' such a thing, no, that I didn't, not for a minute,' said Joshua interrupting.

'Then my only alternative is to assume a belief on your part that she knows something about me— perhaps about my birth'—Guy stopped. The sexton relieved himself by another cough. Guy went on—'There! now you know. Was that what you intended?'

Joshua put out his head to be sure no other persons were near, looked round upon the darkness of the cave, and even felt with his hand its invisible walls. Then he said,

'I told you I didn't know much.'

'You did.'

'Very well. Now, then, I'll tell you all as I do know. 'Twon't take me long. 'Twas you set me off.'

'Me!'

'Yes, when you was down in the vault, you brought back thoughts as I'd a'most forgotten; thoughts as I'd had that night, Lord love us, how many years ago?—when your mother, meaning Mrs. Phœbe,' was down in the vault. Then thing after

thing come to my recollection how she wasted away
and sickened, and how they said she'd something on
her mind; how she was always pushing you forrad
to the squire. Then I began to look to her—Susanna
—and there I see many a thing as set me thinking,
and one or two things as more than set me thinking.
One night I was crossing Tanfield by the workshop
—when I see—'

'Hush!' cried Guy, under his breath. 'She's
coming! I have no doubt you are right. I will
not wait. Keep you close till she has passed. B
sure of that.' He held out his hand.

Joshua grasped it, and then, before letting it go,
said,

'You're welcome to any hints I've give you; but,
mind, I know nothing in a law sense, or aught
o' that kind.'

'Good-by.'

Guy crept up the hill, and began to run across
the heath, thinking to himself, 'he's but a poor
creature after all.'

Joshua stood, shrinking back as far as the wall of
the hollow place under the rock would let him, while

Susanna came nearer and nearer. He saw her slip two or three times, but she seemed to recover her balance with a quiet mind and move on again in a manner strangely unlike Susanna's ordinary treatment of vexations. As she drew still nearer she stopped as though the path grew slippery or wet, and seemed inclined to leave it and advance obliquely up the hill in a direction that would bring her straight to the rock. But the furze-bushes scratched her legs, and she dropped back into the path and went on. She looked occasionally towards the tops of the banks on both sides, to be sure no one was looking down; but, on the whole, seemed to glide through the moonlight not like a living person, but as a dark spectre, who might be supposed capable of suddenly exhaling into the air, or sinking abruptly into the ground, even before the very eyes of the watcher.

But why has she been so long on an occasion so critical?

We must answer that in another chapter.

CHAPTER XX.

SUSANNA'S BOWER.

Guy had been mistaken about Susanna's movements, notwithstanding the carefulness of his
hurried search at the knoll before his own departure; Susanna had *not* then left the house, nor
did she quit it for some time after him. Why she
delayed there, when perceiving matters were so
critical with the squire, we will now explain. In one
of Susanna's many explorations about the fine old
house within the last week or two she had got down
into the cellars, and was surprised to find them so
large, airy, and clean. They formed quite a suite,
opening one out of another. Susanna wondered,
and became very critical in her examination. She
found rusty rings in the vaulted ceilings which
seemed intended to support lamps. The probable
effect of the whole series when lighted up seemed to

impress itself upon her mind as something strange.
It suggested the idea of important assemblages,
or at least of a place of temporary and secret
habitation for persons of superior positions in life,—
for how else could they get here—in this old manor
house? Susanna remembered a tradition of the
neighbourhood, according to which it was said that
this place had been built by the Dalrymples in one
of the periods when religious quarrels ran high and
martyrdom was not unfrequent, in order to have a
place of shelter less known and less exposed to observation than the Hall at Branhape. She went
back to look at the entrance from the steps that
descended from the apartments above. She saw
that that entrance had been closed by masonry,
much of it still remaining; as though it had been
broken through in comparatively recent times by
those who knew of it, but no longer needed it,
as a place of concealment. The secret door had
probably been of wood in the centre of that
masonry.

This was just the sort of incident to excite
Susanna's imagination. She began to enter vividly

into the spirit of the whole ; and then it was not
long before she thought to herself 'this place must
have an outlet to the heath. They'd never be content to be trapped like so many rats, if it got to be
known they were here. I wish I could find the way.
It might be useful.' So Susanna hunted about
with a lighted candle until in the very farthest
of the cellars she saw, she thought, something peculiar in the shape of the ground. Some of the soil
seemed to have been thrown up there loosely long
ago, and never again levelled or disturbed. She
got a spade and dug in it till she felt sure she had
touched a hard substance. Then she delved away
with renewed vigour, and gradually laid bare a flat
iron surface, which, as it became quite cleared from
the soil, showed a thick iron ring. Susan laughed.
Then she wondered if she could lift it. She could
not for a long while—not until she had cleared away
every particle of mould ; then it rose, and with it a
gush of air that extinguished the candle, and left
Susanna in a great though only momentary fright.
She relighted her candle, and managed with many
precautions to descend the winding steps which led

her to a very neatly-finished circular apartment, where there were still on the floor the rotting remains of the superb hangings that had once been on the walls. There was also an oak table, and an oak circular bench or seat running round the table in the centre, still in good preservation. No natural light could ever have reached this place, Susanna thought; but a bronze lamp suspended from the groined roof showed that artificial light had been ready, and no doubt had always been needed when the room was used. Susanna was charmed with her discovery. Here was a place to plot, and to do the many little things she yet might have to do while trying to bring things to her mind. She stepped through the open door into a vaulted passage which went winding about for some distance, then suddenly ended with an iron door, having a very large rusty key still in the lock. After many efforts, she got the key out, cleaned it, put it back and turned it in the lock. Yes, there was the heath, into a little dell of which the chamber opened. Next day Susanna explored the outside of the same spot, which she found with difficulty. Then she saw that the secret passage was directly connected through the dell, with an open water-course crossing the heath in the direction of the village. Still greedy of adventure, and imaginative as to possibilities, Susanna reasoned with herself—'The people of the house couldn't be all hiding at once, for that would have told the story. And those who did hide must have been helped by those who didn't. Or, if it was the squire himself, perhaps he'd want to be able to go up and down by some still more secret way than through the house to the steps that I go up and down. I know! I know!' And Susanna clapped her hands in anticipation. 'I'll lay my life I find a direct way down from one of the rooms upstairs; perhaps from our own bedroom; and if so, I know where—the closet!'

Off she ran, and though to unprepared eyes there was nothing in the least degree suspicious about the appearance of the wainscoted wall, Susanna found a panel extending upwards only a couple of feet or so from the floor, which gave a hollower sound than any other part. She was not long in loosening it, getting it out uninjured, and in seeing a sloping

opening in the thick wall descending directly downwards, which she subsequently found was connected with the suite of cellars.

Susanna almost danced for joy in her exultation.
And of course, she kept her discoveries most carefully within her own breast. She felt sure she would
want them sooner or later, and on the evening of
her marriage she found the opportunity.

When she heard from Guy the news of Mr.
Dalrymple's extreme danger her very blood seemed
for once to get to fever heat in her anxiety lest he
should die, leaving Guy and herself unrecognized.
She was lawyer enough to know that law alone
might prove but an indifferent agency for securing
their rights if the squire did not live to sanction
them, or give before death some testimony to the
world. But how was she to get away unseen—
unchallenged? She was conscious that the critical
moment had come; and that she had two things to
do, while, in fact, she had hitherto contented herself
with providing only for one. No doubt, to have
Guy—her husband—recognized as the squire's son
and heir was the chief thing; but she began to be

dimly conscious that it would be unpleasant, to say the least of it, to bring forth her proofs unless she could explain why she had not brought them forward before. She tried to throw off this new alarm as nonsensical; she tried to persuade herself that they must think her fault venial—that they would say it was only her deep love for Guy, and her fear he might be forced to abandon her by his grand relatives, that had made her conceal her knowledge till the marriage was over. But such comfortings were rejected as useless. Susanna had begun to understand a little of Guy's mind, and to guess from it what might be the mind of the squire as to such deceptions.

All this ran rapidly through her brain as she watched Guy descend the stairs from the dance to go back to the Hall. She had little time for decision, but she did decide exactly as Joshua Darkley had supposed she would—to go at once to the workshop, secure the proofs Phœbe had given to her, and put them into the hands of the squire that very night. Making, therefore, the excuse to the bridesmaid which had subsequently been repeated to Guy on his temporary return to see if Susanna had really gone, she ran to her bedroom, locked the door, threw off her white kid slippers and put on her ordinary boots; then, taking a long dark cloak from a peg, she put it on over her bridal dress, and drew up the hood over her head, covering the fair hair and the wreath of artificial violets; and then prepared to descend through the panel.

She had scarcely got in before she stopped, and returned to the room, murmuring,

'Perhaps it's no good; but I'll think about it as I go through the cellars, so I may as well take pen and paper with me. Is the anonymous letter safe? Oh, yes; here it is.' So saying, Susanna put back into her pocket the letter Guy had received and handed to her, and collected two or three sheets of paper, an inkstand and pen, some blotting-paper, and one of the wax candles which she had bought in honour of the occasion to light up the bridal chamber. With this store she again retreated to the closet; where, turning round to face the room while she planted her feet, she began to descend and to disappear by degrees till her head was on a level with the floor; a moment after the panel slid into its place, and Susanna was gone.

When she reached her 'bower,' as she almost fondly called the round chamber she had discovered, she put the writing materials, and the wax candle, and the lighted candle she had been using, on the table, and sat down on the seat.

She took out the anonymous letter, lighted the extra wax candle she had brought, and stuck it in a cleft of the wood opened by time, and began to examine the document with extreme care. Then she took up the pen, dipped it in the ink, put it into her left hand, and tried some experiments upon one of the sheets of paper. She frowned, and tried again. Still she looked dissatisfied, but again tried, and this time with the right hand. Her face brightened suddenly, as if with new sunlight upon it. Again and again she tried with unfailing success.

'Ah, I see it may be all very well to write with the left hand when you are yourself playing the anonymous, but not when you want to persuade the anonymous out of his own self.'

Susanna laughed, took up a clean sheet of paper, wrote a few lines upon it very slowly, constantly comparing it with the letter before her ; and so thoroughly was she now braced up to her highest pitch of successful achievement that she had no need to make a second copy of the letter she was writing, the one she first wrote was so good.

Susanna held the two letters together, compared them in different lights, and looked quite radiant at last with the conviction of her success.

' Yes, and it's just the same wrong way across the paper as though written by a vulgar sort of person ; and there's his wonderful flourish at the tail of every capital. He daren't deny that.'

Susanna again laughed as she extinguished her lights, left the writing materials on the table, and felt her way along the vaulted passage till she got to the external door, unlocked it, and stood in the deep shadow of the dell, which was made only the more impressive by the fact that there was no snow in that sheltered spot ; and by the intensity of the bright moonlight that flooded the watercourse in the distance, and which could just be seen from where she stood.

It will be understood now why Susanna had been so long in reaching the spot where Guy and Joshua had waited for her.

CHAPTER XI.

GUY SEES AT LAST.

WHEN Guy reached the hedge which extended across the front of the workshop, at the distance of a few feet, he stopped at the gate, for his heart was beating so violently he feared he should burst a blood-vessel or do some other untimely thing before he got inside. He glanced round in the direction Susanna must come, and was relieved to know she was not yet in sight, therefore could not yet have seen him. He got to the window, slid his hand and arm in for the key, found it, unlocked the door, entered, re-locked it, and hung the key in its place. Then he looked round to see how he could best prepare for Susanna's visit. The light from the moon was streaming vividly into the workshop from a skylight on the top and towards the back of the shed, but it seemed only to come in at one window high up, and to go out at the other low down on the other side—the broad one that lighted the workshop by day—leaving all but the window and the intervening roof of the workshop in deep gloom. In a corner of the darkened part stood several planks so disposed —of course accidentally—by Stephen as to cut off the angle from the eye. There was no room to go behind them except by first removing a plank, then getting behind and then restoring it—a process not easy for a single pair of hands, that, however strong, were now somewhat nervous. Guy's position was hateful. He accepted it with a sense of shame that did not promote presence of mind. Still he was there for a great object. He was determined to achieve it if he could; and if it should turn out that he had been deluded by his own morbid fancies, or by Joshua's interference to do Susanna any kind of injustice he would confess everything to her, and let her see it was from no unworthy motive he had so acted.

He was soon completely concealed, and the planks, to Susanna's eye, must seem just as they had been for months past. He had even carefully avoided disturbing the dust and spider-webs any further than he found actually necessary. But could he see? Certainly not, as he stood. He tried in vain to find an interstice. He stooped, and then saw light through. So he began with his fingers to widen the apertures, forcing back the heavy planks, while constantly afraid he might throw one of them down and so be caught by Susanna in the midst of his embarrassment. But, by a sudden effort, he got space at last to see through, more indeed than he wished, and he could now command with his eye the broken pane, the key hanging on the wall, the door, and one side of the shed—the last two being in shadow.

'Suppose the hiding-place be in that other wall,' said Guy to himself. 'I could not watch her go to it, or see what she took from it. I must learn all now.' So he had again to force a space in another part with his fingers between the bottoms of the planks, and was heedless of the pain and injury he experienced till afterwards. But he achieved his object; and thus master of his outlooks, waited in silence for the sound of Susanna's feet.

They came at last—so softly that Guy doubted whether the pressure he heard on the snow could be produced by any human form. He sees a shape darkening against the light window; he sees a hand glide through the broken pane, and move slowly up and down, seeking the rusty key on the rusty nail. Ah! how well he knows that hand, so fair, so thin, so long; of a bluish white; and which he has so often watched with the red light shining through at the nails when near a candle. He can only now see its form, but the rest is vividly pictured before him; for Susanna's hand has long had for him an unpleasant fascination. As he sees it now the wrist does not move, because of the thin sharp points of glass that stick up all round, but is kept fixed and still while the fingers feel about. And he sees those long, snaky fingers turning and twining in the air in search of the key, and throwing their lengthened and complicating shadows on the moonlit wall, like the fingers of some beautiful but revolting monster of the deep in search of its prey. A horrible feeling comes over him to be obliged to own to himself that he does indeed know that white hand—that he has kissed it—that those horrid, creeping, feeling fingers have been tangled in his hair ; that that ring, shining round one of them, has been placed there by him with vows that put his whole future into that hateful hand.   Nor is this Guy's only feeling.   He feels assured in his inmost soul, as he watches his bride with loathing yet fascinated eyes, that it is that hand which has been for years weaving about him a kind of web so quietly and secretly, that he knew it not—suspected it not—till he found himself inextricably entangled.

As he thus looked and looked, he let out the breath that was stifling him in a quick sort of gasp. He was heard.   The hand moved back with a sudden jerk, and caught in the longest point of the jagged glass.   It *did* seem alive then.   There was a little, half-smothered scream that seemed to come from it ; and Guy's excited vision seemed to see in each nail a red eye glaring at him.   He pressed his own doubled hands together on his knees to keep himself still, and to avoid being obliged to withdraw his eyes, or to rush out.

There was a pause of terrible suspense on both

sides. But to his wonder, almost to his admiration for the persistency of purpose it implied, he saw, after a while, the fingers again advance with new caution, even while his strained ears thought they heard the fall of heavy drops of blood on the window-sill, and then the key was safely grasped.

'Now, then—now, at last!' thought Guy.

Susanna unlocks the door, comes in, and stands a moment in the shade, her tall, black form looking like a piece of embodied midnight to the observer; then she moves a little and turns, and the cloak falling back reveals the silver stripes gleaming feebly beneath; another step, and the soft, bright light kisses her fair face, and Guy owns to himself,

'Angel or devil, she is indeed fair!'

She throws off her cloak, which she puts on the bench. Then, just for a moment, she casts one searching glance at the broad window, at the different parts of the workshop, at the planks—where her eye stops for a moment, and Guy's pulse seems to stop with it; for he dares not even dream what the effect might be of their recognizing each other under these circumstances; but the eye passes on, and the form follows its guidance towards the middle of the wall. Guy now sees her place something, he cannot distinguish what, against the wall; he sees her rise higher and higher, evidently mounted on something; he sees her take out what he fancies to be a brick; then, from the aperture thus made, he sees her remove, and hold out into the light, a packet looking like a book in shape.

'There it is then! There is the proof!'

Should he break forth from his hiding-place, challenge her purpose, and compel her to give up to him the evidences so long and anxiously hoped for, and which were now before him? How did he know what fresh complications might yet arise from her plottings if he allowed them to go on? How could he be sure that these proofs were safe in her possession? Precisely the same things that gave Susanna confidence — her own scheming, secretive character, and her belief in the necessity for working slowly towards her aim in the dark — gave to Guy the deepest distrust and alarm. No doubt in one respect — his rights — she must mean to attain the same end as himself; but she might, with her cunning tendencies, err fatally as to the road.

But mingling with this, the first general stream of thought, that flashed as with lightning-like rapidity through Guy's brain, came again the desire to understand his wife's character ; to be quite sure whether she was what he had once hoped, or what he now more than feared. Suspicious as her conduct was in keeping silence about the secret hidden in the workshop until the very night of his marriage-day, when her actions were precipitated by the squire's danger, Guy had yet no certain evidence as to her motives, much as he suspected them. He began to fear his wife's power to deceive him now and for ever, and to leave him a prey to life-long doubts, if he did not keep aloof from her until she should either commit herself to some provable falsehood, or make matters so far clear in self-exculpation, that he might venture to throw aside reserve, and trust to her frank explanations for the rest.

While by rapid gushes of thought Guy ran through this kind of mental communion with him-

self, Susanna stood there before him in the moonlit
workshop, half her form seen in the silvery radiance,
half almost hidden in the deep shade; and he became conscious at last that she must have stopped,
and was delaying for some special reason. Had she
heard him? Had he in his mental agitation moved
without knowing it, and so disturbed her ear? No,
he saw—or rather he partly saw, partly guessed—
that she was stopping to put away the packet safely
in her dress, and then to bind up the wound in her
arm made by the glass. Still she seemed very slow;
and he thought once he heard a sigh, which agitated
him still more, it seemed so full of pain or trouble.
Listening intently, he caught the murmured words,

'What shall I do? I'm faint!'

What should *he* do? Guy asked himself. Feelings of pity began to stir within his breast. He
could not but turn over anxiously in mind every
possible mode of declaring his presence to her
without the overpowering, perhaps fatal, alarm the
sudden knowledge might give. He must do something. Almost before he had made up his mind he
would move, he had shifted one of the planks a

little, and startled himself by the grating noise it
made. In consequence of his movement he lost
sight of Susanna, and was for a few seconds left in
the deepest solicitude as to whether she had noticed
the sound. But when he had again found an opening
through which he could obtain a glimpse of her, he
saw she was still standing in the same place, supporting herself by the bench, her head lowered a
little, and her whole frame quivering—so it seemed
to Guy—either with illness or fright. But presently
her head rose, then her form became erect, and
he heard her murmur in stronger tones than
before,

'O yes, better at last! Thank God!'

And while she appears to be engaged in bandag-
ing her arm with something white taken from her
pocket, probably a handkerchief, Guy sees, or fancies he sees, a tiny bit of cloud fall through the air,
as though Susanna had dropped something. He
could not see anything on the floor—it was too dark;
and he was not sure that the cloud was not a mere
film passing over his own eyes, from keeping them
so long and painfully fixed on one object, straining

through the gloom. But the idea of that cloud, slight as it was, coupled with what he had heard Susanna say, that she was better, kept him to his previous purpose. He thought she might have dropped something that might yet prove of importance in the way of testing her statements as to how she obtained possession of the proofs that she was evidently about to use.

So Guy watched with anxious but determined gaze Susanna's departure with the proof in her possession. He saw the door reopened; saw the tall shadowy form glide through it into the fresh open air and darkness beyond; heard the lock again turn; waited to hear the key drawn out, and to see the arm once more venturing to brave the terrors of the jagged glass in the broken pane; waited, but waited in vain. The key was left in the lock. Guy heard no more; not even the retreating footsteps, which must, he thought, have managed to float over the snow as one does sometimes feel one's feet float in dreams.

In an instant the planks were thrust aside, and one of them thrown down, which fell with a heavy thump upon the bench, then slid to the floor with a repetition of the same strong but hollow noise. Guy flew to the door—yes, it was fast ! He was locked in !

Had Susanna done this intentionally ? At first in his rage and impetuosity, Guy was inclined to say, ' Yes ;' but when he remembered her obvious alarm and suffering through the broken glass, her subsequent faintness, and the extreme agitation she must have been labouring under, he felt he was unjust. He was sure she must either have left the key in the lock unconsciously, or that she was too timid or ill to venture to replace the key through the broken pane, and therefore had left it in the lock, caring no more for the secrecy of the workshop. But there, at all events, he was— fastened in, and condemned to stay the whole night through, unless he could either break the door open or resolve to destroy a portion of the window-frame. While hesitating as to which of these last courses he should adopt (the idea of submission even to a temporary confinement was not, under present circumstances, to be debated for a moment), he recollected the cloudy something he had seen drop through the air. Judging as well as he could of the precise distance from his hiding-place where he had seen it fall, he went down on hands and knees, and felt about among the shavings and chips on the floor. Almost the first thing he touched was a paper, which seemed to be a letter. No doubt this was what he had seen fall; but, to make sure, he continued for a minute or more feeling about him, but discovered nothing else.

He rose to his feet, got into the pale stream of moonlight, and looked at the paper. It was a letter and he could faintly trace an address upon it. But the imperfect light baffled all his efforts to read. Once he thought he saw his own name; but when he tried to follow the curves of the letters they faded, and when they reappeared seemed to be just whatever he chose to make them.

Guy felt and looked at the letter. It was evidently open; it had, therefore, never been sealed, or had been sealed and then the seal been broken; but there was no wax. Guy could neither see nor feel any remains of wax outside; but, on lifting the outer fold, he felt inside it a little round roughness, as though a wafer had been used, but had dropped off. Could he not get a light? Stephen used to keep a tinder-box here. Guy went about exploring one dirty, dusty corner after another, and at last found the crazy, worn-out tin box. There was a flint and some matches on the top, but no steel. He lifted the inner lid, and put his finger to the bottom. Yes, there was some tinder remaining; but whether it would prove of any use, after lying there so long neglected, he could not tell. Again groping, he brought out from a corner a rusty axe, and, after arranging the thick back in a sloping position over the tinder, he began to strike at it with the flint. It was weary work. He thought he should cut his knuckles to pieces uselessly. It was but seldom he could extract a spark, and when he did succeed, he could not make the spark reach the tinder, or else the tinder was worthless and would not kindle. He was about to push the whole apparatus aside in anger when he saw a gleam. Down went the flint from his hand.

He stooped, blew gently, the red glow widened and widened; he applied the match, it flamed; but how was he to read the letter? He had no candle. Invention is keen at such times. He drew towards him, with a sudden sweep of his hand, all the dry chips lying on the bench, and then, setting light to them, he found he had a capital blaze. And thus Guy read the following letter :—

'If you'll go to Stephen Waterman's workshop, and take out a brick in the right-hand wall—the eleventh brick, counting downwards from the top, and the fifth, counting on a level line from a nail with a big round head—you'll find a packet. Take it directly to the squire, who is ill—perhaps about to die—and it'll greatly benefit your husband. But mind you, for his sake, don't let him or anyone know how you discovered this. I ask this as my only reward for doing both of you a great service.

'A Friend.'

We need not say by whom or under what circumstances this letter had been written; or how wonderfully Susanna's luck had aided her cunning, when she was able to drop such a letter within sight of Guy, at so critical a time.

Guy's first act, as soon as he had read it hurriedly through, was to heap more chips on his little fire, which was expiring. Then, as the flame revived, he held the paper close to it for a moment, and then he cried out,

' It is—it is the same hand! Joshua, the rascal! is playing with us both. No wonder he knew she had gone to the workshop. Why, it was the vagabond himself who sent her here! Yes; this is decisive! My wife is innocent!'

He began now to cast about for means wherewith to extricate himself. The thing was not in itself difficult, if Guy chose to disregard the subsequent exposure. But he did not want to draw the neighbours' attention to the workshop. He felt all over the lock. When his fingers touched the keyhole, he felt the round part of the key—its cylinder—slightly projecting. He almost fancied he could grasp it between his fingers and turn it round, but of course laughed a moment after at his own

absurdity. But there might still be tools in the
workshop that would help. He remembered a pair
of nippers that Stephen used to lend him in his
boyhood, to play with while watching operations
in the workshop, and which had been left among
others to Guy to furnish his own toy-toolbox. The
box was there still; perhaps the nippers also. He
found them; grasped the edge of the key, and by
his great strength and his closeness of grip was able
to turn it round. He was then at liberty.

Having locked the door and restored the key to
its place, he stepped past the cottage into the
village, and made way slowly towards the Hall,
wondering how Susanna would proceed when she
met the squire face to face; and not sorry, now
that he was satisfied of his wife's honesty, that the
squire should know the whole truth from her in
the simplest and most natural manner, and without
the agitation of Guy's presence. Guy could not
bear the idea that the noble face, now so full of
bodily suffering, should look even for a single
instant doubtfully upon him. It was torture—the
mere fancy, that his own dear father should, at the

very moment of recognition, begin by a suspicion that the claimant was either a drivelling fool or an impudent impostor.

'Well,' said Guy to himself, 'I'm glad I'm satisfied about my wife, and can now satisfy those who will have a right to question her.'

While he was thus thinking, thus passing along towards the crisis of his fate, he saw, at a place where another road branched off from the chief one that Guy was pursuing, a carriage come out of the former, and pass rapidly on towards the Hall just in front of Guy.

'Surely,' thought he, 'that was Mr. Morgan's carriage! A moment sooner, and I might have accompanied him. I fear this betokens fresh alarm—fresh danger. Is the squire about to make his will, or to alter it?'

CHAPTER XII.

Mr. Dalrymple lies, or reclines, on a low bed
in his drawing-room, where he has caused himself to be placed, in order that, while bedridden
for so many days or weeks, as he fears he shall be,
he will keep off as far as possible the depressing
associations which prolonged confinement in one's
bedroom is apt to create. Into this room Mr.
Morgan is introduced by the servant.

'Ha! Morgan, is that you? I am glad you've
come. Thank you for overlooking the untimeliness
of my request. You wonder to find me here. Well,
I don't mean to give in—not this bout. We are all
of us,' added the squire, with a sudden change
of voice and manner, and an upward, reverential
glance from under his thick eyebrows, 'subject to
His disposal. Don't think me so weak or so wicked

as to forget that. No; but if there be one truth in life clearer than another as to man's duty it is this—Do your best for yourself under all circumstances, and then you may pray with a safe conscience for God to help you. That's my creed, and I'm not going to change it because of a broken bone. If I am called to-night, I shall have only too many sins to answer for; but I am very sure He won't make it a sin in me that I keep a cheerful mind, and say frankly I want to live if I can, so long as I have no reason to be sure I am about to die.'

Mr. Morgan was a man of the world, and used, therefore, to trouble in all its forms; but the great respect, almost affection, he felt for the squire, after so many years' tolerably close intimacy, made him fear his voice was growing husky, and his eyelids wet as he answered,

'No doubt of it, sir; no doubt whatever. But how was it? I have heard nothing but what your own brief, hurried note told me.'

'Why, you know, young Waterman was married to-day. I have been waiting only for that event

to send for my niece; so I wrote my letter yesterday, and sent it off, and to-day, like an old fool
as I was, could not help, in sheer gaiety of heart,
going to join the hounds for a last run. Heaven
help me! there's no doubt it will be my last run,
perhaps for reasons I didn't just then expect. Well,
I managed to send the gout to the devil—much
good may it do him!—got on my boot, took my
very safest horse (I was careful as to that, you
may be sure), and set off. But the day was so fine,
the sun so cheering, the run so good, my brother-
sportsmen so kind and genial in their congratulations, and I felt altogether so buoyant—such
a sense of renewed health and happiness, that I
forgot what it was to be getting near to eighty
years of age; and when we came to a low stone
wall, with a brook the other side, I could not do
as the more staid respectable gentlemen of the
party did—go round by the gate and bridge at the
end of the field; no, I must do as I had always
done before—go over it. And I did go, with a
vengeance, and cleared the wall well enough; but
when the horse alighted on the muddy sloping

ground beyond the wall and stream, he slipped, threw me, and rolled upon me. That's the story, and here's my leg—bandaged, as you see.

' But, come, you'll be glad to hear that the surgeon thinks there's no real danger. Some hours ago he was inclined to give me up. He didn't say so, but I saw his look at Guy, and I heard them whispering together afterwards when they thought I had gone off in a dangerous kind of sleep.'

' I am indeed thankful to hear that,' said Mr. Morgan. ' And now, as I am sure you ought not to exhaust yourself with conversation, permit me to ask what I can do for you ? '

' Yes, come to business! About my will. It must seem strange to you that I have never before consulted you on that point. But it happened thus :—My estates, as you know, were entailed on my son, if I had one, and were at my disposal in case of the failure of the direct line. Had my son and wife lived, I intended to have bequeathed my personal property of every description to my widow: both would thus have been provided for. But the

shock of my great loss left me for many years
unwilling seriously to think of new modes of disposal. Of course, I did make some sort of pro-
vision for my niece. Here is a will—pray don't
laugh at it, or look professionally serious about it,
for you may be sure it was no distrust of you, but a
freak of mine, the preparing it myself and keeping
it unknown. I want you now to see if it is good
for anything—if it will hold.' The squire handed a
sheet of letter-paper to Mr. Morgan, who perused it
carefully twice over, then said,

' Yes, I think it's all right. Why, squire, you
ought to have been a lawyer!'

' I thought I had managed it well,' replied the
squire, with a smile illumining his hollow and faded
but still red cheeks. ' But I must tell you the
truth. I had an old family will before me, made
by Judge Dalrymple, who, to his eternal honour be
it said'—and again the squire smiled, and somewhat roguishly—' threw overboard in his own case
the circumlocution so dear to his humbler brethren,
and made a single sheet of paper like this contain
all he had to say.'

'Of course,' retorted Mr. Morgan, 'he hadn't much that he wanted to say?'

'No; and that's exactly my case. A few legacies to my servants, an annuity for Mrs. Hammett; a personal remembrance for Guy, with a recommendation of him to the future owner of the estate; ditto, ditto for yourself and partner; certain rings, jewels, and books to personal friends among my brother magistrates and neighbours; and everything else to Lucy Dalrymple—that's the upshot of the business. So now is it right—will it do?'

'Perfectly. And if I have yet said nothing as to my own or my partner's share in the matter, it was not because I did not feel, and feel keenly, your munificent kindness, but simply that I did not choose to dwell on it till I had answered your business question.'

'That's just like you. Always doing the right thing in the right manner. Morgan, give me your hand. I am not usually very demonstrative, but, if it will be any satisfaction to you to know from me in plain English what I think, I will say this, you are the very model of my notion of a lawyer!—that

is, upright, well-read, experienced, and of unerring
sagacity in tracking roguery of every kind.   There
—there's no romance in my opinion, is there?'

'No,' said Mr. Morgan, laughing as he returned
with cordial interest the squire's friendly grasp,
'but it's the truth—at least I hope it's the truth.
I meant it to be the truth when I began business
many years ago.   Excuse one remark about the
will.   I see there occur in it words, more than once
repeated, with reference to the possibility of your
wife and son being still alive.'

'No, no, you misunderstand,' said the squire,
who looked almost as confused as a bashful boy at
the mistake.   'I—I thought at one time (not for
long, I assure you) I ought to marry again, and
then —'

'Oh, of course.   Excuse my remark.   It would
have been a great omission if you had not done
this; but I thought you might have had some more
special idea.'

'No, no; that was all,' said the squire mourn-
fully; and his thoughts were evidently going far
back into the past.   'No,' he resumed, 'the boy,

you know, was brought back dead, and now lies with his and my ancestors; and, as to my wife, I could not doubt Phœbe's distinct statement that she saw the whole sad business go on—saw her mistress drowned right before her eyes!'

'Well, Miss Dalrymple, I hope, will yet be able to comfort you.'

'I hope so too. She comes to-morrow. Hark! What's that? A ring at the bell. It's too early for her. I didn't choose to ask her to come on the wedding-day, but she's probably just so near that she might get here soon after midnight if she were to hear of my accident. Be so good, Morgan, as to go and see. You know not how I long to have her once more in my arms, since the fright I got some hours ago that she and I would never again see each other. I felt it easier to die than to die without again seeing my niece.'

Again the bell rang, and this time as boldly as before it had seemed the reverse. Mr. Morgan hurried out, hearing the squire again call after him,

'It can't be her; but if it is, tell her I'm better, and let her come to me at once.'

But it was not Lucy.

Mr. Dalrymple had lain back on his pillow, thinking of her with a smile on his face some five or six minutes, when he began to hear voices in angry altercation.

The door was ajar, and he could recognize both Mr. Morgan's and a servant's voice, but that of the third person he could not remember, though it seemed disagreeably familiar.

'I tell you I must and will see Mr. Dalrymple,' said that voice.

'And I say you can't and won't see him,' replied the servant. 'I've told you three or four times I was ordered to keep everybody out.'

'Let me pass. I must see him. If he is dying I must see him.'

'What is it? What's the matter, John?' Mr. Dalrymple called out impatiently. 'Who is it you are talking to?'

'Why, sir; it's a person, sir, as as forced her way in; I'm trying to get her out, sir.'

'Don't let anyone come in, Morgan, please,' said Mr. Dalrymple fretfully, as the lawyer entered.

'My good young lady,' Mr. Morgan said, turning back, 'do pray let them take you to the housekeeper. You really can't come in here. The squire cannot and will not see you this evening.'

Mr. Dalrymple could not see anyone enter because of the screen before the door, but he thought the voice was inside the room when it next spoke.'

'O yes,' it said; 'I'm sure he will see *me*— the squire will see *me!*'

'Morgan,' he said angrily, 'take the woman away.'

Then the voice said, very loudly and distinctly,

'Tell him Mistress Dalrymple wants to speak to him.'

The squire gave a cry, and started up in spite of his injured leg, supporting his weight against the table, and by his hands resting on it, with his head stuck forward, staring at the door.

A minute more and Susanna in her bridal splendour stood before him, looking at him with a cold triumphant smile. She held out the packet and waved her hand a little as a sign to him to open it.

The squire opened the packet, and found a book and a letter. He had scarcely given a single glance at the last before he cried out, in a voice of the deepest agitation, his hand trembling as he held the letter with it,

'What's this? Where did you get this? Merciful Heaven, what revelation is this coming to me from the grave! Speak, woman! Where did you get this letter from,—'tis my wife's?'

'I got the packet, sir, just as you see it, from Stephen Waterman's workshop just now.'

'Stephen Waterman's workshop?' asked the squire, in growing amazement. 'What, hidden there by Phœbe?'

'I don't know, sir. A letter was put into my hands this evening between the dances—I couldn't see who it was—that told me to go to the workshop, and described the place behind a brick where I should find this.'

'Where is that letter?'

'I have it here, sir,' said Susanna, beginning to

search first in one pocket, then in another, but without success. 'I'm—I'm afraid I've lost it,' said Susanna, shrinking a little under the eyes of the squire and his companion, and showing how much troubled she was by this inability to explain her actions properly.

The squire, however, had forgotten her by this time. He reclined on the low bed, with the letter still unopened on his knee, but the book—a Bible—open; for he had found there a tress of hair, and his eyes were filling with tears, while his heart was beating at a fearful rate. It was almost as if he lacked the courage to open the letter, so long did he leave it unexamined. But after a pause he took it up and looked at the still unbroken seal, and said to Susanna,

'Do you know the contents of this?'

'No, sir.' Susanna said this so artlessly, and looked so fair and innocent, that the squire wondered at himself for supposing she could have anything more to do with the matter than the performance of some duty that had fallen into her hands.

And so at last he broke the seal (one that he

knew well), and began to read the following
letter :—

> ' On board the " Black Gull,"
>> ' Wednesday Evening.

' *I am settled in the ship, Godfrey, and Phœbe
leaves me in a few minutes. I hear the impatient
cries of the sailors, whose boat keeps knocking against
the side of the vessel just where I write. In a few
minutes I shall be alone. I am very—very miserable.
I don't know why; for, after all, it is not much to
cross the sea once in a lifetime. I did not think so
when I crossed it with you (to go to your home and
all that I am now leaving), and I cannot tell why I
shudder at it now. Yet a fear has been over me, ever
since my foot left the land, that it would never touch
it more. But I do not sit down to write to you of
this, but of our child. Oh, Godfrey! my own best-
beloved husband still, in spite of all differences of
faith, I have determined it shall be as you wish.
Phœbe goes not alone. She shall take him presently
away with her—away from me, but to you ! Do you
now forgive me ? Shall we not now meet again when*

*I return, as our hearts have so long told us we ought
to meet ?*

' *Poor Phœbe ! Now that she has lost—*'

What ails the squire ? Why are his hands
shaking so as they hold the outstretched letter ?
Why does he look again and again at the words
that have so overwhelmed him ? Why does he
faintly gasp out at last, without taking his eyes from
the fatal lines,

' Morgan ! Here ! Look at this, and tell me if
I read rightly, or if my senses are—' Mr. Morgan
drew near, and read the words to which the quivering forefinger pointed. He read, ay, and read
again and again before he, too, would believe.

' Aloud ! Read them aloud,' murmured the
squire. Mr. Morgan read—

' *Poor Phœbe, now that she has lost her boy, she
clings more than ever to our sweet darling. Say a
kind word to her, will you not? and let her see him
often.*'

Mr. Morgan stopped, but the squire said in tones
that trembled with passion,

'Go on—you! I cannot!' Mr. Morgan obeyed.

' *There, then, I have promised; but how shall I—
Oh! how shall I part with him, my darling boy? He
is lying on my neck now, with one little hand twisted in
my hair and the other stroking my wet cheek. Perhaps he wonders why it is wet, as he looks up at me
with those eyes of yours. He little thinks it is because
when I have folded this I shall lay him in Phœbe's
arms—perhaps never to take him back. Who can
tell? How tightly he has twisted his hand about my
hair. When Phœbe takes him I will cut off the
piece as he holds it, and he shall bring it to you in
his hand. It will show you a little, perhaps, how he
is twined about my heart, and how much of that—the
best— will be dragged and torn away from this ship
to the shore, as I see him there in Phœbe's arms, and
the miles growing and growing between us.*

' *I have taken the cross from his neck—you know
what that means—and have bought from our captain
one of your Bibles—a very pretty one, you see, with
bright clasps, that he may take to it early. Try,*

Godfrey, to realize what it is I give up to you, and think of me, then, as you once used.

'*Phœbe has come, and my trial—and I have not said one-half that I wished to say. You will not forget to be kind to Phœbe.*

'*Farewell! Would that I had never begun this journey. Ever, my own dear, noble husband, your affectionate,*

'AMY DALRYMPLE.'

As Mr. Morgan finished reading the letter with measured, weighty tones, and awe-stricken face, the squire again undid the rusty clasps of the Bible and took out the knot of hair which he had replaced. He understood now. Yes, there it was, dark and tangled. You could fancy the little stubborn fist had but just let go of it.

A mist began to gather over the squire's eyes. Presently he said,

' Where is he? Oh, my God!—all these years, and I not to know!'

And the old man's stout heart gave way and he fell back, trying ineffectually to conceal his grief.

Mr. Morgan merely said, in reply, 'I will despatch the servants in every direction for him;' and went out.

And Susanna and the squire were now left alone together. But he had forgotten her very existence. He lay with his head back on the pillow, his hands across his face, and his great frame heaving up and down convulsively.

Mr. Morgan found them in that position when he returned, Susanna still standing near the bed, and gazing with half-shut but inquisitive eyes upon the stricken squire.

'Will you excuse me, as Mr. Dalrymple's legal adviser, asking you a question?' said Mr. Morgan to Susanna.

The eyes opened widely. Susanna had not previously guessed the vocation of the gentleman she had found with the squire. She did not seem pleased with the discovery; but, after a pause, she replied,

'What is it?'

'I understood you to say you knew nothing of this till to-night. Pardon the question—I mean no offence—but was that really what you said?'

' Yes, sir,' said Susanna.

' It would be very desirable for—for the welfare and comfort of all parties if you would be so good as to mention—to recollect—some kind of proof of the fact.' The squire who had by this time mastered the first wild gush of emotion produced by his wife's letter, now raised himself on one arm and looked at her with a kindly smile.

' Lawyers, you know, my dear, always will be lawyers. So, come, speak to me. He means, and no doubt he is quite right, that we mustn't let ill-natured people say or think that you concealed this for your own ends. Make it clear to us ; that's all he wants.'

' Oh, sir ! ' exclaimed Susanna, clasping her hands piteously together, ' if I have done wrong in any way please to forgive me ; but I declare, in the presence of my Maker, I did not know till now how great a secret I was bringing to you in that packet ! '

' And you say you have lost the letter that told you where to find the packet ? ' asked the squire, with growing distrust.

' Yes, sir ; but I will try to recover it ! ' murmured Susanna, glancing the while aside towards the open door where she saw the shadow of a man projected in a listening attitude.

'There is your letter, Susanna. Thank God it fell into my hands,' cried Guy as he came in and gave her the letter. Then he darted one quick questioning glance at Mr. Morgan's face, and then looked slowly round towards the squire.

'Guy,' said Mr. Dalrymple quickly, 'come here.'

Guy went and stood by him, and Mr. Dalrymple gave him his wife's letter, and watched him while he read—watched him yearningly, with tears rolling down his cheeks into his white beard.

Mr. Morgan turned away, and did not again look round till Guy had placed the letter back on the pillow, and taken up the hair, and laid it tenderly on the back of his hand, as if it were too silky and delicate to touch with his workman's fingers. Then he laid that back on the pillow too, and Mr. Morgan thought—

'The hand has brought the hair at last, then— but it has grown and roughened a bit on the journey.'

Mr. Dalrymple took both of Guy's hands, and looked up into his face, waiting to see the change come over it. But the change was long in coming. Guy seemed to shrink more and more into himself. What was he?—a workman again. It seemed to come back to him—the old life—the life of so many years—all at once. What was he doing there, with his rough hands lying in Mr. Dalrymple's? Was he dreaming? he asked himself; and as he thought it might all be a dream, a mist came over his eyes, and he felt dull and stupid.

Mr. Dalrymple let go his hands, and holding both arms out, he cried,

'My boy! my boy!'

Then there was a cry from Guy, hoarse and strong, and a heavy fall that shook the floor; and somehow Mr. Morgan, when he had seen the kneeling Guy, with his head strained to his father's breast, with his cheek on his mother's hair and letter—somehow Mr. Morgan found himself flattening his nose against the opposite window in a most extraordinary and unlawyerlike manner.

CHAPTER XIII.

FATHER AND SON.

For a long time father and son remained in the position they had first fallen into—Guy on his knees, with his arms wound round the squire; the latter on his low bed, holding Guy by the neck as he stooped over him, and detaining him with hands fondly clasped together, and that knew not how to let go. Breast to breast together heaved and fell. The unacknowledged sympathy each had previously felt for the other was now understood, and grew in the brief space of moments into deep, unutterable love. Both forgot for the hour their respective sorrows, and gave themselves up to the sway of this new and holy passion, with all its happiness and sense of complete repose.

Susanna, at a hint from the lawyer, had withdrawn with him ; so there they were, father and son, left alone together ; and might feel, think, or speak just as they pleased. But they did not at first seem to want to speak. Life—so fast ebbing away from one of them—seemed to have told them all that they just then cared to know. 'My son!' 'My father!' these were the all-sufficient communications between them; and even these they expressed far more truly to themselves and to each other by their silent and prolonged embrace than by the utterance of the words.

But at last the happy and yet sad squire, who felt at the same moment the presence of the brightest sunshine and the blackest shade he had ever known, began to relax his grasp, and allow the head to rise a little so that he could look at it, and presently he murmured,

'Yes, it's Amy's boy, sure enough. Guy, how long have you suspected this?'

Then Guy told all about Phœbe Waterman's death, and his pictures in the fire. And to all his father's fierce bursts of anger against her he answered with earnest entreaties for forgiveness.

'Forgive! What! can *you* forgive her, Guy?' asked the squire.

'I do indeed, as God is my judge.'

'Oh, but I cannot! All these years to have been left alone, while you lived near me, knowing me, yet not knowing me; I knowing you, yet not knowing you! Oh, Guy, lad, God help me! I do not know whether I am most happy or most miserable! If I had but had you for ten years, nay five, I should have esteemed myself the happiest man in creation; but now, when my years are so narrowly measured, when even months may be too large a reckoning— Oh, boy, this is hard to bear, very hard!' The squire fell back on his pillow exhausted, for his wound and want of sleep were seriously increasing the evil of so much mental agitation.

Guy followed him with his eyes and with his affectionately clasping hands, saying little, and divining, almost before the squire spoke, the nature of the emotion that moved him.

'Ah, Guy, how proud I should have been of you! I could have forgiven Phœbe the loss of a few years, if it were only for enabling you to show the true

stuff of which you were composed. Yes, my boy,
I honour you all the more that you have been a
workman, been poor, been subject to a thousand
temptations, and yet come out, to my own full
knowledge, an honest man, and, in every vital essen-
tial, a true gentleman.

'Won't the doctor be angry with us both for all
this?' asked Guy.

'Tell him I don't find a son every day.' Seeing
Guy's half smile at the revival of the squire's
ordinary mood, he added, 'Yes we will make the
best of his absence and of his ignorance of what is
going on, for I own he is likely enough to be despotic when he does come again, and he may, perhaps, divide us for a bit.' Then turning their talk
into a new channel, he said, abruptly, 'About your
wife?'

'Yes, sir,' said Guy, with constraint, and there
stopped.

'Of course you are quite satisfied she did not
know of this till to-night.'

'I—I think not.' The squire noticed the pause.
Presently Guy hurried on—'The letter I found

shows that she had been suddenly told, as she said, to go to the workshop.'

'How came that letter into your hands?'

Guy had not been prepared for this question; but it was impossible to have reservations from the squire, even though they related to his wife and to his own suspicions of her. So he told to the wondering squire the whole history of the first anonymous letter; and then of what had happened from the moment of his receiving the long-expected second communication to his seeing Susanna find the proofs in the workshop: including his adventure with Joshua Darkley.

'Is it at all possible that Joshua told you the truth; and that he, therefore, could not have written the second communication?'

'I think not, the handwriting was so obviously the same —'

'Stay! Is not that of itself suspicious? If the same man was pursuing the same secret system of friendly aid, why should he not acknowledge himself to be the same?'

'But I do not remember any actual discrepancy

between his letters to her and to me, except in the fact of his writing first and twice to me in a sense apparently hostile to my wife, and then writing to her when the real secret was to be suddenly disclosed. But in truth, my dear father (this was the first time Guy ventured the word, and both of them lost the thread of their converse for a second or two in the sense of the sweet strangeness of the sound)— but in truth, my dear father, I am but a bad hand at concealment of any kind, and I am sure it cannot be necessary. You will, for my sake, be as kind and considerate towards Susanna as—'

'Never fear that, my boy; but let us know the whole truth, or rather your whole thought.'

'Well, then, I have been much shaken by many things that have happened of late—mostly trifles. And when I saw Joshua's warning about her motives so strongly confirmed, to all appearance, by his correct and timely direction to me to follow her to the workshop last night, I scarcely knew how to keep down thoughts that I have since been sorry for. For, while I was in the workshop, I had a very striking proof of her innocence afforded me. It proves that the last and all-important communication was not written by Susanna herself, as I fear you must at first have suspected—'

'I did, particularly when she was obliged to confess she had lost the letter,' interposed the squire.

'While hidden there unknown to her I saw her come. She got the key through a broken pane of glass, and cut herself badly in doing it. This made her afterwards stop a minute or two in the workshop, when she had obtained her prize, to bind up her arm. She then pulled the letter out of her pocket with her handkerchief, and it dropped on the floor. Of course, so far as she knew, it was in the highest degree improbable that anybody would believe her subsequent story if that letter were not forthcoming. She thought it was lost. You thought so too, and began to judge her. But, providentially, I was myself the secret witness that she dropped it accidentally in the workshop. I cannot, therefore, resist— I mean I am bound gladly to avow my conviction that Susanna did receive that communication from some one else, and that she had not previously known anything of the secret.'

'I am glad, Guy, to hear you speak as you do, if I do not myself, as yet, imitate your example. So one question more—is it clear that Susanna knew nothing of your intended visit to the workshop?'

'Quite; I have not the remotest doubt upon the matter.'

'And equally certain that while you were both in the place together, that no movement, or sudden breathing, or gleam of wandering light could have revealed your—or some one's—presence to her?'

'I—think—not,' answered Guy slowly.

'I must own she would have been something above or below ordinary women if she had, while so engaged—alone, in darkness—made such a discovery and yet been able to plot so brilliant and decisive a stroke to extricate herself at the instant of her alarm. And the very possibility of this depends on a previous fact — that she had previously written the letter, and kept it ready in her pocket.'

'I do remember,' added Guy, with obvious pain and reluctance, as if ashamed of his own thoughts, 'that I did twice make some slight noise, and that on the first occasion I feared she cut herself through

that cause.   But then she went on and did the whole
business afterwards.'

'A brave wench, anyhow !   Well, and on the
second occasion ? '

'It was through a movement I made which caused
me to lose sight of her for an instant, and when I
was able again to obtain a glimpse of her form she
was leaning—and I thought tremblingly—over the
bench.'

'Ah !'

'Yes; but then I heard her murmuring to herself
about her faintness through the wound, and asking
what she should do.   And beyond these things,
which seem to me quite explicable, I saw nothing
to raise a shadow of doubt as to her being entirely
ignorant of my close neighbourhood.'

'Did she return the key through the pane ? '

'No.   She was either careless now that the
proofs were removed, or she was too nervous to
venture her hand once more through the broken
glass.'

'Then she left the door open ? '

'No, I was locked in.'

'Ah!' The squire smiled, but it was in an odd, grim kind of manner, that made Guy uncomfortable. After a pause, the squire remarked,

'One last question, boy. Have you ever seen in your wife any tendency to scheming? Has she got that kind of thing in her at all; or can you say she is absolutely, unmistakably free from all such devilry?'

Guy's face became greatly discomposed. He did not reply for some time, though the squire remained patient, for he saw his son was trying to speak. At last Guy said,

'I don't know. I cannot answer that exactly as I could wish. *But she is my wife.*' These last words were uttered in a low tone, and with bending head, that rendered it quite unnecessary for the squire to pursue his questions.

While the pair were trying to forget the painful thoughts raised by the conduct of Susanna, Guy noticed his father look with an anxious glance at his leg, then at the door, as if wondering how long the doctor would be before his next visit, which he had promised to make in the course of the evening.

Guy understood, and begged to be spared while he ran down to see if he could learn anything about him.

He went out, thinking only of his father, whose suffering and danger now seemed the chief things he cared for in the world ; but the very instant he got out upon the landing, and began to descend the stairs with their skirting—the gilt balustrade—and to glance down to the rich tesselated pavement, faintly gleaming below, he was recalled to himself and his position. Was he now the future lord of this place ? Were those his servants whom he would presently meet? Did they already know—would they salute him with—his true but as yet unheard name ? Lucy too, would she be here on the morrow — lost to him for ever—yet conscious, like himself, that but for his own act, her love might now have crowned his wonderful lot? Then he asked himself, where was Susanna ? And at once all the wild and wandering flights of his mind stopped. Guy never dreamed within her atmosphere, except, indeed, when he happened to be able to forget her presence altogether. Meeting with no one to speak to, and hearing some commotion in the courtyard behind the house, which he thought would annoy and injure the squire in his present feebleness, he began to explore his way through a corridor. Ah! how well he knew it! How well he remembered his last long-lingering clasp of that unresisting hand, when he parted with Lucy on the ever-memorable night of his discovery of Pample's guilt! But the noise increases. There seem to be many feet and many voices, which he can hear ascending some neighbouring staircase. What can it all mean? Violence—and to the squire? Impossible! What then? He knows not—cannot even guess. Nor can he find any door opening to the place where they are. He runs back, thinking he has missed the road. Surely the noise comes now from the very entrance-hall through a gallery by which he had descended. He reaches the hall. The noise is upstairs—possibly in the very apartment of the squire. He runs up, half-frenzied with alarm, yet fierce with the idea of his father's danger, and the inexplicable intrusion upon him. The noise increases at every step. He bursts into his father's room, the drawing-room, and is greeted at once by a rapturous shout from the assembled crowd.

Dazzled and dizzy with the unexpected gleam of so many eyes; trembling with emotion, he sees them all gathering round him—men and women, old and young, the squire's large family of domestics, who have already heard the news. And with them are several of his tenants, who, while passing homeward from the wedding, have caught the wondrous tale, and many of his labourers living near, or happening to be at the Hall; making together quite an assemblage, who cannot be kept quiet, but must see both the old squire and the young one—'God bless them both!'

Again and again broke forth the cheers, the squire himself leading them with flashing eyes and glorious voice that might in other days, in the field of battle, have cheered an army, and saying between whiles to Guy, as soon as the latter managed to get to him,

'It's all my doing. Just when you left me two or three of the servants came to tell me what was wanted. How could I refuse? Besides, I want

everybody to know I recognize you beyond all possibility of question as my son.' Then turning
away from Guy he raised his hand, and when the
enthusiastic storm began to lull said, as the voices
all subsided into deep silence, ' Friends, this is a
proud day for me, and I hope for you.'

' It is! it is! God knows, squire, it is!' responded one of the tenants.

' Yes, friends, this is my own true and lawfully-
begotten son, who was lost and is found. You all
know the story. I cannot talk much now. But let
us wait and trust in God's goodness, and then you
shall, I hope, yet meet us both together in some
hearty thanksgiving feast. Meantime, there is my
son, as true and noble a gentleman, I do believe, as
the Almighty ever made ; and you will confess I
ought to know a little about him ; for I knew him
long before I knew how near he was to me. I
respected him—I honoured him—as plain Guy
Waterman ; what, then, shall I do now that I call
him before you all by his rightful name—Guy
Dalrymple, — the undoubted heir to my name,
ancestry, and estates ? '

We need not say how the squire's tenants, domestics, and labourers answered this question ; or how difficult it was once more to allay the excitement the squire had raised anew.

'There, friends, I thank you with all my heart. Leave us now.   I hear the doctor's ring; and he will make me smart for neglecting his injunctions.'

CHAPTER XIV.

THE LADY OF BRANHAPE.

WHEN Susanna left the drawing-room with Mr.
Morgan, that gentleman, to her great satisfaction,
took his departure. And then her first oc-
cupation was to go from room to room wherever
she could find one unoccupied, and gaze yearningly
and delightedly on all she saw. She found on the
landing a beautiful little silver candlestick, with a
wax-taper burning. With this she went about,
handling the silk curtains to feel their rich, soft,
glossy texture ; passing her finger tips to and fro
across the exquisitely-beautiful inlaid work of
chairs and tables; sounding musical instruments
that she sighed to think she could not play—'not
yet at least'—as she prudently reminded herself:—
—a harp that had never been touched since Mrs.
Dalrymple ('Guy's own mother'—Susanna thought,

with new sense of the relationship) had played it; and a piano which Lucy had incessantly practised upon.

If she came to a cabinet it was wonderful with what almost childish enjoyment Susanna opened it, drawer after drawer; but always suspicious, no matter how many she found, of other and secret drawers hidden somewhere behind. But the treasures in them! How shall we paint Susanna's boundless delight to come upon almost inexhaustible stores of gold and silver coins, each of them evidently worth far more for its history and age than even for its precious material; rings and gems of all kinds and colours, ruby and green, and some of them flashing with diamond light; rare ivory miniatures of members of the Dalrymple family, painted by one eminent artist after another, through several generations; and hosts of other things, the very names or uses of which Susanna could not even guess, though she was sure of their great value.

A girl, the daughter of an old and sick domestic, happened to be up, and came to inquire about the wandering footsteps. She curtsied slightly as she saw Susanna, thinking her perhaps the visitor of some other servant, and was passing on. But Susanna stopped her promptly.

'Do you know who I am?' asked the supposed visitor, towering proudly above the girl, whom, indeed, she scarcely seemed to see.

'No, if you please,' was the reply, a little less assured than before.

'Then understand, and tell your fellow-servants, that I am the lady of Guy Dalrymple, Esq., who is now, where he ought long ago to have been, with his legitimate father.'

How wide the little girl opened her bright blue eyes, how suddenly and eagerly she bobbed down to the floor, and continued bobbing even when Susanna had stalked grandly away; and how, when at last she did venture to take her eyes from off that awful and beautiful and majestic figure, and forget the terrible mistake she had made, she ran as fast as her excited mind and excited legs would carry her to tell her sick mother the wonderful news, and call up the rest of the servants, we need not further dwell on; but it was thus Guy's presence and true character became first known among the domestics.

Susanna next began to stop before the great gilded mirrors, looking at herself now in this attitude in one mirror, then in that in another, and producing yet a third effect in the next; and so continuing, and always with smiles of contentment. And, certainly, it is a charming picture that she sees this moment in the narrow mirror over a console-table between two windows. She has thrown aside her cloak, and stands there in her bridal dress, troubled only by the unseemliness of her walking-boots, which she knows not how to change, till she dimly remembers that she had intended to put her white kid slippers in her pocket when she set out on her mysterious expedition. Yes, they are there after all! How fortunate! In an instant the boots are thrown off, and Susanna feels once more every inch a lady. It was wonderful how those boots were beginning to trouble her; yet now the trouble is happily removed.

And for some time, with her toilet thus completed, she examines herself in the glass. Who shall say what new dreams are buzzing in that active brain? What visions of court, and court-dresses, and of kissing the king's hand, and of being talked of for her beauty beyond all the other beautiful women there, and of the admiration of tall and nobly-born and richly-clad gentlemen—grand and beautiful gentlemen—who must seek to win her favour, and who would not be like Guy, so cold; and who might, if he didn't mind, make him jealous. Ha! ha! ha!

Yes, Susanna laughed at that part of her vision, and turned herself half round, while her head inclined to take a sidelong survey of her tall and graceful form. And she thrust out the slender foot and ancle, and endeavoured to judge of their effect to other eyes. And then again she laughed before finally sobering herself to her wonted mood.

And it was very remarkable that Susanna was sure to be thinking about some very bold and unscrupulous stroke of stern business when she gave way to these bits of anticipatory personal enjoyment. Thus was it now.

It will be remembered that Phœbe, in a kind of passing suspicion of Susanna's possible conduct, had written on the cover of the Bible a plain acknowledgment of her guilt, and of her confession of it to Susanna. It will also be remembered that the latter had been obliged very suddenly—almost within sight of Guy himself, as he remained below stairs in attendance on his (supposed) dying mother —to conceal the knowledge of the writing from Guy; and yet be so able to conceal it as not to raise any alarm in Phœbe's mind as to her motives, if she again looked at the Bible. Susanna had, therefore, gummed the edge of a flyleaf with such neatness and accuracy as to fasten the leaf almost without seeming to have intended to fasten it; she had thus hid the dangerous writing; and yet was able, by a touch of her penknife, to show Phœbe that she had done it for the moment only, so that Guy might not accidentally discover it till Phœbe chose that he should learn the truth, either through her own disclosures, or, after her death, by Susanna's agency.

That Bible was now in the squire's hands; would be handled by him and Guy, and perhaps by the lawyer, and who could tell by how many more ! If the actual looseness of the leaf, through its temporary fastening, were suspected, the place would be at once examined, the leaf set free, and the writing discovered. Susanna had never till now felt how serious this was. Blinded by her one predominant notion that sucess was the be-all and end-all, no matter how obtained, she now, that she had succeeded, began dimly to see, as we have previously remarked, that her principles and views were different from the principles and views of her husband and of the squire. Vague notions began to grow over her of what they meant and believed by the words ' honour ' and ' truth.' She almost fancied she would herself have to grow truthful and honourable in more than outward seeming, now that she was so very rich and grand. But certainly this Bible promised to be for her an ugly beginning, if she could not extricate herself from the threatened danger. She must think what she will do.

CHAPTER XV.

WHILE Susanna was still hesitating as to the best course, Mrs. Hammett, whom she had not yet seen since her arrival at the Hall, advanced to meet her with a respectful curtsy and smile. Susanna looked at her in return with an expression that was meant to be condescending, but which seemed to the housekeeper at once so silly and so insolent, that she felt her cheek and neck crimsoning with anger; and she had to put a restraint upon herself, and to remind herself that the squire could not do without her at present—that she must bear whatever Susanna chose to inflict — before she could summon up resolution to say,

'I beg to congratulate you, madam, and also Mr. Guy, on this great discovery.'

'You are very good,' was Susanna's tart reply;

'but may I ask you to show me which rooms will be most suitable for myself and husband?' Mrs. Hammett bit her lip, bowed her head, and turned to lead the way.

They went at first into a wing of the building, and Susanna was conducted into a very charming suite of apartments—a bed-room, sitting-room, and an ante-chamber, all connected one with another, and with an external staircase.

'Perhaps, ma'am, you will like these rooms. They were arranged in this manner some years ago, when the squire had some distant relations, a married lady and gentleman, who were invalids, staying with him for some time.'

Susanna scarcely looked at the rooms, but went to the window and looked out, then went to the door, and, after a pause, she said, pointing,

'Is that the room where the old squire is now lying?'

'Mr. Dalrymple is in quite another part of the house,' replied Mrs. Hammett, with pointed emphasis on the words 'Mr. Dalrymple.'

'Oh, that is sufficient. Of course, we should

wish to be near him. Please to show us some rooms
where we can readily get to him.'

Now Mrs. Hammett had received a hint from the
squire that he would not care how far off she
managed to select rooms for Susanna and her husband. He knew he could have the latter with him
when he pleased, and he wanted to know that he
would *not* have the former when he did not please.
But the hint had been a very faint one : for the
squire was too full of good feeling, and too sensitive
as to his son's position, to let any noticeable confession escape him of his belief in Susanna's unwor-
thiness. So Mrs. Hammett, finding she could not
evade the plain directions now given, and aware she
would not be justified in attempting to oppose them,
again moved forward on an errand of inquiry as to
where Susanna was to be lodged. Room after room
was looked into and rejected — whether because
Susanna did not like them, or because she was getting nearer, with every rejection, to some wish or
thought of her own, Mrs. Hammett could not understand.

'Is there no bed-room in the same corridor

as the drawing-room and the other chief apartments?'

'Only the one that we call the state bed-room, which was fitted up for a royal princess, who slept here one night in the last century.'

'Let me see that.'

Mrs. Hammett went to the door, opened it; and although the single candle carried by the housekeeper revealed only partially the splendour of the place, Susanna was smitten at once.

'Open the curtains,' said she. Mrs. Hammett obeyed, and the light of her candle was just strong enough to bring out all the characteristics of the bed, without exposing the faded tints. Susanna's greedy eyes saw only the thick yellow satin curtains, the gleaming of the golden cornice, the royal arms, and the delicate blue of the silken counterpane. This was, indeed, a bridal bed! Not in all her dreams had she realized anything so magnificent as this; not, at least, while keeping within any reasonable limits of probability. She scarcely cared to look around on the noble wardrobe, the marqueterie cabinets, the deep closets, the beautiful little tables with vases and other articles of the most delicate porcelain, exquisitely painted, or on the glowing pictures on the walls, which were, perhaps, rather too glowing, for the taste of the last century was not fastidious.   But not even these pictures could draw Susanna's eyes from the splendour of the semi-royal bed, one that had actually been graced by a princess, and that was now to be hers.

Ay, hers!   However much Mrs. Hammett may be surprised, Susanna determines this shall be their bridal-chamber; and she quietly tells Mrs. Hammett so, with the additional remark, as she looks out of her half-shut eyes,

'I wonder you did not show me this before.'

'But, excuse me, do you think Mr. Guy will approve?'

'Of course he will.   Surely he can leave all that to me.   At least, if he does not, I presume *you* can.'   Susanna gave a stately bow and a delicately venomous smile as she said this; and Mrs. Hammett was obliged to acknowledge herself silenced.

'I saw you pass one door in coming to this that you did not open; the very next, I think, to the drawing-room, where the old squire—I mean where Mr. Dalrymple—is.'

'Yes; it's locked,' said the housekeeper, turning away as if she had an idea she was not expeected to say any more.

'Mrs. Hammett!' sharply called out Susanna.

'Yes, ma'am?'

'Will you be so good as to remember that I will signify to you when I wish you to go, as well as when I wish you to come?'

'Very well, ma'am.'

'If that door be locked, you have the key, I suppose, and can open it?'

'But I don't think the squire would like that room to be used. It is Miss Lucy's room, and she is expected to-morrow.'

'Oh, indeed! Well then, permit me, if you please, to see it.'

Mrs. Hammett's genial, kindly temper had never perhaps been so strongly tried before. Every word from Susanna, every moment spent with her, only deepened in the housekeeper's mind her sense of disgust, and her desire to give the new mistress sudden and short notice of her departure. But she knew how much the squire depended on her; she knew, too, how impossible it was to worry him just now by any discussion on the subject; so, for his sake, she must bear patiently. While thus feeling towards Susanna, she had long felt that the two persons in the world whom she loved the best were the squire and Miss Lucy; and these were the very persons whom she feared Susanna was bent on outraging, if only she could do it with safety. It was, therefore, with a very ill grace that Mrs. Hammett managed to find the key of the door, and open it. And then she had the surprise of finding that Susanna, instead of looking, as she had expected she would, with an envious eye and a biting tongue on the boudoir of her rival, was in an ecstasy with the room, with everything in it, and with the taste displayed in the fitting it up. It seemed even to make Susanna forget her supercilious dislike of Mrs. Hammett, for she turned quite graciously upon that lady, smiled, and said to her,

' Pray, did you help to get all this into such a very delightful state?'

' Well, we did it between us—the squire, Miss Lucy, and myself; but it owed most to Miss Lucy. She is—'; but there the speaker stopped, wisely suppressing the complimentary remark she had been about to make.

' Do you know, Mrs. Hammett, I really think that I must take possession of this dear little room till Miss Lucy comes; and then I shall tell her how charmed I was with it, and that I waited here to welcome her back to it.'

Mrs. Hammett said nothing, though she thought and felt a good deal. But Susanna did not allow her to lose much time in unprofitable ways. Seating herself in one of the low armchairs, while admiring its colours of white and gold, she said,

' Well; this room evidently needs nothing to be done to it. It's quite perfect. But I must beg you to put plenty of servants into the state bedroom, so as to have the fire lighted, and the whole thoroughly aired and made comfortable in an hour or so. You will see to it promptly? Yes? I thank you. Tell my husband, when you see him, where I am. That will do.'

Mrs. Hammett curtsied, and withdrew. The moment the door closed after her, Susanna leaped up, clapped her hands, and said to herself,

'Can't I play the lady! Oh, that my poor and very clever mother might but see me! I wasn't a bit frightened of her, at least, not after the first minute or two. But now for that confounded Bible! I won't sleep in that grand bed till I have done something to feel more secure. I don't know what yet. But I have got near to him where he lies; and now I must wait, and watch, and plan. One last stroke only, and then I shall be in no danger of nasty reproaches from either of them.

'So this is where Miss Lucy—' this was said aloud, and the last two words with an expression that we cannot even hope to convey to the reader; 'This is where Miss Lucy used to sit and dream about Guy, and wonder who I was, I suppose; and what sort of a person I might be. She'll know soon, but I'm afraid she won't like me.'

Susanna rose with a laugh, looked at herself in a little mirror, took off the wreath from her head, put it on again, and then once more reluctantly took it off, saying,

' Yes, I must make myself for an hour or two as little conspicuous as I can. But I'll put it on again by-and-by. I'll take care everybody knows who I am to-night, and what night it is. That I will! Ha! there are the bells! They know then in the village what has happened. I must take care to give Joshua a timely hint. Yes, I'll thank him for his second letter. And I'll give him so many reasons for believing he did as I say he did, that the cunning old fellow will be sure to be quiet. Nobody knows better the buttered side of his bread than he does! How madly the bells do ring! As though trying to trip one another up in their joy.

She was interrupted by a gentle tap, and the opening of her door and the entrance of a servant, in what seemed to Susanna gorgeous livery, with a tea-tray and various little delicacies. When he had gone away Susanna could not sufficiently admire the beauty of the silver service, or of the blue and gold earthenware, so exquisitely thin and fragile-looking. But her thoughts soon changed.

She opened the door noiselessly, and stood for
a moment listening if she could hear any passing
footsteps ; but as she did not, she crossed the threshold, and again paused. The drawing-room was
next to her own, and it was open, and she thought
she heard low voices murmuring within. She drew
nearer with stealthy step, carefully observing in
every direction that she was not herself observed.
She could at last distinguish the voices—Guy's, and
then the still deeper and more ringing one of the
squire. If she could but hear what they were saying ! She pushed the door very gently till it was
wide open ; and then, with head and ear bent back
towards the speakers, while face and eyes were
turned in the direction of the landing and the gilt
balustrade at the top of the staircase, dreading
every moment to see some form emerge from below,
and confront her, she heard at last :—

'O yes, that sleep did me good. I am better
now. But you, my boy, why don't you go and get
some rest ? You are strong ; but you don't know
yet how much I may have to tax your strength, so
you must husband it for my sake.'

'I could not sleep; no, not for anything the wit or wealth of man could promise me by way of temptation. I feel as though I shall never be able to sleep again—I mean I am so wakeful.'

'Where is your wife?'

'In the next room, I believe.'

'The next? What, Lucy's?'

Father and son looked at one another. Could Susanna have seen as well as she was able to hear, she would have noticed a dark frown of anger pass over the squire's face; while, mingled with the same kind of manifestation on Guy's there was a reddening tinge that showed how vivid and full of emotion were the associations raised by that name. The squire knew, without further explanation, that Guy, when he spoke, had not had the remotest idea that Susanna's present abiding-place had been previously Lucy's own room.'

'About fetching Lucy, Guy? I'm afraid she would never forgive our leaving her where she is all night—I ill—and you just become known to us. I hope I shan't get worse before to-morrow, but I might. Well, well, boy—I won't say that again if

it hurts you. But as to Lucy? Mrs. Hammett
wanted to go off for her as soon as she knew of my
mishap. But I said " No." I incline now to think
Lucy should be here. If so, don't you think you
ought to fetch her?'

'I?'

'Yes. You know she is your cousin. You ought
to be the first to inform her of your claims upon me
and upon her, and to break to her, poor girl! about
this cursed accident.'

'Yes,' said Guy, but it was evident he spoke
hesitatingly.

'Come now, boy, honestly, can you or can't you
trust yourself? You know that you can never now
love her except as a sister, which she may and
ought to be to you. Your position is decided. It's
too late to think what might have been. Be a
man in this, as in everything else. Take Mrs.
Hammett with you. Let her first meet Lucy while
you keep out of the way. Let her tell enough to
introduce you, and then in half-an-hour the worst
will be over, and you and she will both be glad.
Can you do this?'

' I think so. But are you sure we can both be away from you so long as three hours?'

'Oh, yes; I can doze again; and you know we both promised the doctor we would do our best to cultivate sleep. Reach me up your mother's letter. Thank you. Now the Bible. I want to be alone with these for a time; 'twill do me good.'

' Then, my dear father, I will go to fetch her. Yes, you are right. I ought to go. I will go.'

Susanna thought it time now to go too, before her husband discovered her as a listener.

CHAPTER XVI.

THE SEED SOWN COMES TO FRUIT.

'WILL Guy come to me before going to fetch Miss Lucy?' Susanna asked herself, with something like a jealous pang at her husband's indifference on this their bridal night. He did not come. She heard him rapidly descend the staircase, as though he had even speculated on the possibility of meeting Susanna if he did not get quickly away.

What should she do? The squire was alone in the next room, and the Bible was in his hands or resting on his body, or deposited within reach, close by his side. Should she invent some errand to go in and get into conversation with him, and trust to her wits to enable her to get hold of and carry off the Bible, if only for a few minutes? She had determined, with her usual promptitude in action when action was indispensable, what to do if only she could so get hold of the book. She would loosen the edges of the leaf, get it open, erase Phœbe's writing from the cover, and then gum or paste the whole leaf down so carefully and effectually that it would be not possible to remove it afterwards. Thus, she would have a double security. The writing itself would remain unsuspected—unthought of, so long as the leaf was let alone; and if by any means unknown to Susanna the leaf should be released by other persons and the marks exposed, it would still be impossible for anyone to say what the writing had been, or to prove that Susanna herself had had anything to do with the erasure. She had provided the gum ready in her pocket in anticipation of the need.

But how could the Bible be got hold of? Clearly not with the squire's knowledge and sanction. The very suggestion, no matter how ingeniously made— no matter how skilful might be the pretence— would be sure to raise anew his suspicions of Susanna; and induce him not only to guard it with renewed personal care, but to re-examine it with eager suspicion. That idea, then, must be dismissed. What next?

Why, there remained but the hope of her being able to remove it while he slept. But how was she to know when he waked or when he slept? Susanna's foot kept rapidly patting the floor in the impatience of her thoughts. The difficulties seemed insuperable. She could not venture, amid all this blaze of publicity, among so many servants, what she might have ventured in her own cottage in the village. She might be exposing herself at every step to watchful and unfriendly eyes.

And yet she felt driven on by her fears to do something, even though it were necessary in so doing to venture much. Her very presence in the Hall—the atmosphere and look of the whole place —seemed in some undefinable way to whisper a warning to her, the lady of Branhape must not be proved a cheat!

She was angry with herself that she had not earlier guarded against this danger, both as regarded the Bible and as regarded some happier fable in explanation of her own knowledge of the mysteries of the workshop. She had better have burnt the Bible at once, as she had often thought of doing; but she had been restrained by her cunning fear that the proofs might not be esteemed sufficient if she lost any portion of that which Mrs. Dalrymple had confided to Phœbe. Then again the letter spoke so strongly about the Bible as to make its loss a great cause of suspicion! No, she could not blame herself for keeping the Bible.

While reflecting thus, and yet at the same time employing her busy hands in examining the many little treasures that Lucy had gathered together, she heard the sound of the squire's cough. She felt sure it was him she heard, though the sound seemed very distant. She wondered that she had not heard anything of the kind before; but in an instant she saw what had happened. She had, while rummaging about in the alcove (from which Lucy's birds had been removed for the time by Mrs. Hammett, in order that she might the better attend to them in her own apartment), opened a door, hoping there might be a communication that way with the drawing-room which adjoined; but, seeing it was only a kind of enclosed cabinet for curiosities, she had thought no more of it, and left the door still open. It was through this place, hollowed out of the thickness of the wall, she heard the squire's cough. The thought flashed across Susanna's mind, 'Can I not from that place watch him, and so know how to act?'

To any woman but Susanna this would, under present circumstances, have been a hopeless undertaking. She 'could not,' as she said laughingly to herself, 'ring for one of the gorgeously-habited servants to bring her a gimlet,' or its equivalent in some more disguised shape. No, nor could she expect to discover any kind of tool in Lucy's room that would serve her purpose. But Susanna had on two or three occasions found a small gimlet so exceedingly useful that she had long accustomed herself to carry one about with her — properly guarded—among many other matters not usually discoverable in a young lady's pocket. Susan Beck had always done so, and her admiring daughter did not lose sight of so valuable a precaution. So, fastening her door (she 'would say she had felt fatigued, and wanted to sleep a little if any one came '), she began operations in a dark part of the cabinet. She supposed the wall behind the ornamental woodwork would be brick, and therefore difficult to get through; but what if it were stone? Why, then, her plan would be a failure. To her great satisfaction she found that the back of the cabinet was, in fact, a small door that had once opened from the drawing-room, but been closed to ensure ' Miss Lucy ' greater privacy. The woodwork was, therefore, quickly bored through. But the gleam of light was so small and the wood so thick that Susanna could see nothing through it. Then she made other holes, close by, until she managed, by the aid of her pen-knife, to break them all into one, and find her industry and perseverance rewarded. She could just see at the farthest part of the room from her, the low bed, and the squire reclining upon it, and the lamp beyond, throwing a bright light upon the patient.

Susanna was now so far prepared.

About one o'clock, as well as Susanna could

calculate, Guy and ' Miss Lucy ' might be expected at the Hall. Before then she was determined to be safe from exposure as to the deception she had practised for so many years with regard to her secret knowledge of Guy's true birth. It was now just ten o'clock, as she saw by the golden timepiece that a fair nymph on the mantelpiece was holding up, and which Mrs. Hammett had set going, so as to see if it was in proper order, among her other preparations for Lucy's return. Susanna had, therefore, just three hours. In that time everything was possible. And so she kept going to the hole and fixing her eye restlessly upon the squire, conscious that for some time her watchfulness was thrown away, as he was not even trying to sleep. He lay there with the Bible in his hand, and the letter on his breast, looking towards the soft light of the lamp, as though reflecting or feeling too keenly to allow himself to re-examine, as he had intended, these precious memorials of his wife, which were scarcely less dear to him for her sake than for the revelation they brought with them—that his and her son lived !

But after a while he began to look at the bit of

tangled hair; to feel it, as it were, film by film. This went on for a long time, interrupted only by a hasty dash of the hand across the eyes at intervals. But at last he replaced it between the leaves of the Bible, not, however, until he had reverentially put it to his lips. He then began to read once more his wife's letter. Susanna thought he would never have done with it. She wondered if he was trying to learn it by heart, he was so slow in getting through it, and he looked away from it so often, with his eyes turned up towards heaven.

But when he had finished his perusal, and had endeavoured to remove from his face the traces of his grief, he seemed to be experiencing a change of feeling. He moved restlessly; he glanced towards the spot where Susanna's eager eye was fixed upon him, as though he was thinking of the inhabitant of Lucy's room; he took up the Bible, and began to turn over the leaves in a hasty, inquisitive sort of way that made the heart of the watcher flutter. Then he put his hand to the bell on the little table by his side, but paused with it uplifted in the air, and hesitated, and finally put the bell gently back without call or warning. He had writing materials at his side. He began to handle these with the same uncertain kind of touch. And again Susanna saw the look towards the room where she was, and felt sure she was in some way or other the subject of his thoughts.

He took some writing paper from a case, and by the aid of the latter rested upon his knees began to write. It was evidently a short note, for in a minute after he folded it up and pulled the bell-rope, this time without the least sign of hesitation. Susanna saw a footman enter, receive the note, look at the address, bow, and go away, all in dumb show, for not a sound of the conversation could reach her. She tried once whether, by ceasing for a moment to see what was going on and putting her ear to the hole, she could hear and distinguish what was said; but she could not. She heard some low, faint murmurs of voices; that was all.

But when the servant had gone away the squire turned, placed the Bible on a little table by his side, and seemed about to compose himself to sleep. The note, therefore, was not to anyone in the house, neither was any immediate answer expected, or (perhaps) practicable. To whom could he have written? Susanna's fears pointed to Mr. Morgan. The squire perhaps was sending to fetch him back to the Hall, although he had but lately gone away, and it was now getting late. She thought of this, and the mere fancy that not only the Bible, but she herself, might yet be subjected to his close investigation, nerved her to do and dare everything rather than have her glowing and beautiful future spoiled by exposure at the last moment.

Eleven o'clock! The squire has never been still for five minutes together. Susanna cannot even hope he is asleep. On the contrary, he once more stirs and rings the bell. Again the servant enters, and she sees him go to a table, pour out some medicine from a phial and take it to the squire, who drinks it. Susanna hopes it may be a sleeping-draught. She has heard Guy say the doctor had given the squire a medicine of this kind, which he was only to take in the event of his being very restless. This incident gave her new confidence to wait yet longer before confronting the alarming question — what other course could she adopt in time?

Susanna feels angry now with the noisy village bells which, though at a considerable distance, are yet heard distinctly, breaking out from time to time in fresh gushes of enthusiastic joy. They may help to keep the squire awake.

Twelve o'clock! Susanna has not for the last fifteen minutes withdrawn her eye a single instant from the hole, and during all that time she has not seen any kind of movement on the part of the squire, except the regular rise and fall of his breast, which she sees, or thinks she sees, going on. The squire must be asleep.

She would like to wait and watch yet another quarter of an hour, but it is too dangerous. In an hour Guy and Miss Lucy will be here, and it is far from impossible that Mr. Morgan, if it is he whom the squire has written to, may precede them; nay, may even now be hurrying his horses across the park in obedience to an urgent call.

Fortunately for her purpose there are great silence and solitude all about the drawing-room door.   No doubt Mrs. Hammett has ordered everyone to keep away, so as not to disturb the squire in case he might sleep.   Susanna thinks of this, and it makes her bolder in risking detection. She gives one searching glance all round and over the gilt balustrade down to the hall below, and she stands for a single instant in mute, listening suspense; but that is all.   One minute she was standing in the cabinet, the next she was inside the drawing-room door.

She saw at the first glance something that considerably helped and reassured her.   There was a screen in the centre of the room that completely shut off the squire and the low bed he lay upon from her observation, and which of course, therefore, rendered her first movements invisible to him if he were to happen to wake.   No doubt it had been placed there by Mrs. Hammett's kindly care, in order to help the effect of the great fire that was burning not far off in the splendid grate, and which Susanna could see just beyond the line of the edge of the screen.   This was a great auxiliary.   Here was a place from which Susanna might safely reconnoitre and advance when she saw opportunity, and to which she might make timely retreat when danger threatened.

Putting to the door behind her so that no mere passer-by should see her crouching behind the screen, and gliding with velvety softness of step across the carpet, she took up her post so near to the squire that she could hear his breathing, which was heavy and troubled. Her penknife again was put in requisition to cut a small slit in the unresisting portions of the surface of the screen, and then Susanna was able to survey closely the field of operations. The squire was evidently asleep, though by no means in a sleep that promised security to Susanna. Even if she got the Bible safely away, it was not at all unlikely that he would wake and miss it before she could get back, and the exposure would then be the more prompt and decisive. But that was a risk that must be submitted to. So the only question was how to get hold of the Bible as quickly as possible, get the damning sentences erased from the cover with a rapid and not too nice hand, gum down the leaf, dry it, and replace it in some incredibly short space of time. That was the programme. And Susanna, with just one spasm of fear affecting her breath, prepared for action.

There was a table close by the squire on which were the writing materials previously spoken of, and upon which Susanna supposed the Bible also to be; for she could not see it. The squire, in addressing himself to sleep, had pushed the little table (which moved easily on castors) out of his way as he turned in that direction. It had therefore got a little behind him—at least so it seemed when looked at from Susanna's position.

She must now, then, venture beyond the screen. But even in that she was fortunate. If she went out on the right side of the screen, towards the window she thought—nay, she was sure—he would not be able to see her without making a sudden and considerable turn of his body, which he was unable to make in the broken and bandaged state of his leg. Of course then, it was just within the bounds of possibility that even if he were awake Susanna might leave the screen on that side, go round behind the squire's bed, reach the table and

take the Bible from it, return to the screen, get away
from the room, fulfil her task, and replace the Bible
in exactly the same way. Susanna did not delude
herself with much hope on this score if the squire
was fully awake; but the mere thought of what
was possible, both as to his state and her own skill,
strung her powers to the very highest pitch; and
strengthened her by the assurance that if she could
do the whole so successfully as scarcely to arouse
his attention if partly awake, she was thus taking
the precise course to secure success if he were
really asleep, as she had no doubt he was.

Never, perhaps, before did human form move
across a space so apparently independent of the
laws of gravity and the results of motion as Susanna
moved now. With breath held in, feet rising and
falling mechanically one after another, the arms
bent, and the hands drawn back to the breast, the
head bending low, and the eyes fixed on the sleeper,
Susanna achieved her perilous transit in safety, and
reached the back of the bed. But while she was
eagerly scanning, inch by inch, the number of steps
she had still to make to put her hand on the Bible,

and while she saw with some dismay that the book was clearly within the range of the sleeper's eye, she heard him say,

'Anybody there?'

If a stroke of paralysis had been sent through Susanna's frame she could hardly have experienced a greater shock. He was, then, awake; or, worse, she had waked him, notwithstanding the wonderful softness of her every movement. She glanced back despairingly at the screen. No; she must not venture to move. Absolute stillness was her only chance of escape.

He did not speak again; he only sighed. What a relief that sigh was to Susanna. He had been disturbed, but was not suspicious. But what was she to do? Wait there till he slept again? The idea was torture. The golden moments were flying fast, and ruin would come upon her if she did not now succeed. Susanna no longer deluded herself with the idea that she might brazen out full exposure. She was quite aware that neither Guy nor his father could be dealt with in that fashion.

Minute after minute thus passes in deep silence.

He must be going off again, he is so still. No ; he stretches out his hand, draws the table near, and takes up the Bible. Despair is in Susanna's heart, and not despair only, but something still more terrible, the shadow of which she yet only vaguely sees, and does not at all acknowledge.

Again the squire examines the Bible in the same peculiarly-inquisitive manner that had so alarmed Susanna a little before. He looks at the first fly-leaf before the titlepage, holds it up to the light from the lamp, turning a little round that he may the better do so. He turns over the leaves in order to examine other individual leaves in the same way, and Susanna partly sees, partly guesses, that they are the leaves between the different books where blank spaces occur in the printing, that he examines so intently. At last he comes to the end, where there is no flyleaf, but where *there ought to be one,* as Susanna's conscience hastens to inform her. He holds up the cover of the Bible—the very cover that contains the precious secret ! Susanna trembles as she wonders if it be at all possible to see writing through the fly-leaf which she had so ingeniously fastened down. But she dares not wait another moment. The position has come for which she has all along been preparing. She must now present herself before and speak to him. But not thus. No, she must get back, and come freshly, and as if for the first time, into the room. Away, therefore she goes, gliding with the same noiseless step as before, but with greater rapidity; she passes behind the screen, pauses there one moment to repress the beatings of her heart, and then, an instant after, she is back in her own room.

Back, and dropping in a state of deadly faintness into the white and golden armchair. She had scarcely touched the refreshment which Mrs. Hammett had sent her. Now she paid the penalty of her previous excitement. She stayed thus for a few minutes, vainly contending with the terrible sickness. She tried then to move, but could not; and so yet other minutes passed before she was able to rise, go to a little side-table, and pour out, with tremulous hands, a glass of sherry, which a servant had brought in just before her beginning work in the cabinet. She drank the wine off, and ate a biscuit or two, and they seemed to bring back her courage and physical strength.

Half-past twelve! One half-hour only left. But has she even that time? She hears something which, to her sensitive apprehension, sounds like the roll of wheels on the gravel at no great distance. Straightening herself to her full height, looking just for one moment in the mirror to see that her smile is set to the right point of effectiveness (and she is obliged to own that it persists in a certain ghastliness), she opens and shuts her door with an ostentation of noise, advances to the other, knocks with careful respect, hears the loud

'Come in!' and she goes in, and steps before the screen right into Mr. Dalrymple's view. He neither smiled nor spoke, but waited in grim wonder.

'I hope, my dear sir, you are better,' said Susanna, advancing still nearer to him, 'I have been waiting for hours in the hope of my being called in to help you; and so, as I really grew too anxious to wait any longer in suspense, I have ventured to intrude unasked.' Susanna smiled one of her most winning smiles as she said this, but the squire bluntly said,

'Thank you, but I'm not in want of anything Mrs. Hammett and Guy do all for me I can possibly wish.'

'But you must allow me, as your son's wife—' The squire winced at this, either with bodily or mental pain, but Susanna took no notice, and went on.—'Yes, you must allow me to give you your medicine, or to read to you or to watch by you. Now, my dear sir, I am sure you must not talk. I must be your doctor till Guy comes.' So saying, Susanna began to bustle about, and presently to touch the table whereon, however, no longer lay the Bible.

'Well, since you wish it, take a chair and sit down. I wish to have a little talk with you. I have, indeed, sent for Mr. Morgan to be with us while we talk. But I don't want to frighten you. I do want the truth.'

'The truth?' gasped Susanna, still trying to speak in her artless tone, but not able altogether to manage it.

'Ay, the truth. I will tell you honestly many fears have crossed my mind about the time and manner of this discovery. I can't beat about the bush. I tell you plainly you must try to clear yourself from the foul imputation that you knew of my son's birth before you married him, and fraudulently concealed it till after the ceremony.'

'Oh, my dear, dear sir,' Susanna began to whine.

'Stay; one moment more. You are young. You may have really loved Guy, and, not knowing what true nobleness is, may have feared he would desert you when he knew the truth. If so, confess, and let us make the best of a bad matter. I do not tempt you by any promise. I do not at this moment know what my son might in that case say or do, and I ought not to commit him in his absence. But this I say, it will be a thousand times better for you to acknowledge the truth and repent the deception than to have your guilt discovered by other persons, if you are guilty.'

'But I am not! I am not! I am not, indeed!' pleaded Susanna, going down on her knees, and looking up to him with streaming eyes. 'Oh! I should have been base, indeed, so to have deceived one like Guy, so noble, so trustful! Oh, it is cruel in any one to think so; most of all in you, sir.'

'LIAR!' shouted the squire, in his most tremendous tone. 'Look here!' He held up the Bible, and Susanna saw Phœbe's writing all exposed. In that brief absence of hers from the room he had run a sharp penknife all round the edge a little within the fastening gum, and, of course, the concealing leaf was loose, the hidden writing exposed to the world!

At this moment there was the loud sound of wheels followed by a ring of the bell.

'There they are! There is Guy, your deceived husband, but husband of yours no longer.'

'You will tell him?' hissed Susanna, drawing nearer the squire, who looked at her face and was startled into sudden silence. An instant after he laid hold of the bell, but Susanna's hand was upon his. Again she hissed,

'You shall not, I warn you. Would you make mischief between man and wife?'

'Dare you threaten me in my own house? Here!

Guy! Guy! Help!' While the squire thus shouted out, Susanna's quivering hand clasped him suddenly by the throat; there was a wild struggle, the squire's almost insane rage injuring him far more than Susanna's convulsive attempts to stop his cry, until he dropped suddenly back, and moved neither hand nor foot again.

'Is he dead?' murmured that now terrible voice. 'Have I killed him? No, no, no, I only meant to —to.' But she stops. Guy will be up in a moment. She glances at the squire,—at his throat. She sees no mark. She is safe, then. Snatching up the Bible, she flies back to Lucy's room.

There, with a hand that seemed endowed with a superhuman facility of rapid execution, she scratches out word after word, measuring the while, second by second, the number of seconds she may yet have in which to complete her task before she hears the eventful steps ascend the staircase.

It is done—not so neatly but the signs of erasure are there, and faint, very faint indications of the writing itself. But it must do. But the leaf? What can she do with that? The gum will be wet for some time, and so reveal instantly to the first observer what has been done. She had calculated on time to dry it. There is only one alternative— to tear it out and to scrape off the slender strips of the edges of the fly-leaf, left by the squire's penknife, still fastened to the Bible cover. That, too, is accomplished in less time than it takes the reader to follow our words. She runs out; she hears people coming; she steps into the squire's room, almost throws the book on to the senseless body, and so escapes — just escapes — back into her own room before Guy and Lucy ascend the staircase.

CHAPTER XVII.

LUCY'S RETURN.

WHEN Guy and Mrs. Hammett reached the inn at the little town that had been appointed as the meeting-place, Mrs. Hammett got out from the carriage to seek Lucy. In a few minutes she returned, saying,

'Poor child! I left her all in a tremble. But she knows who you are, and why you come. Shall I go in again with you?'

'If you please,' responded Guy, after a moment's hesitation. So they went in together.

Lucy advanced with timid gait, and glad, though tearful, eyes, saying to Guy as she put her hands in his,

'Oh, Guy, is it true?'

'It is! It is!'

'And my uncle—your father?'

'Is better, and waits you so impatiently, that I begin to think he cares more for his niece than for his son,' said Guy, trying to smile, but making a melancholy affair of his attempt at pleasantry. Lucy responded both to the attempt and the failure very much in the same way. And then there was a painful silence.

'Come,' said Mrs. Hammett, 'we must be quick.' So, leading the way, and holding in her hands whatever little articles of Lucy's personal luggage she could find, they went to the carriage, and were rapidly driven off.

From time to time, Guy, though he could make nothing more than a spasmodic attempt at conversation, which never came to any useful end, managed to glance at Lucy, desiring to see if she was altered —to judge how she had fared during her long absence —and with what feeling she was returning to Branhape, after so prolonged a stay at her own proper home. He soon settled one thing, that she was very much more beautiful than he had ever before thought her. Her colour was a little paler than of old, but then the expression, always Lucy's great charm, had wonderfully improved. The eyes, too, though dim with tears, were so eloquent, sweet, and bright, that Guy felt to resent the change, and became almost jealous as to the cause. Something, he thought, must have happened at her father's, to enable her to come back and look so altered for the better. And, once that thought fairly established in his mind, it was extraordinary with what skill and almost magical power he traced it out through a thousand imaginary details, until he had made himself as wretched as he could possibly desire. Then he began to reflect on what he was about, and to smile bitterly at the absurdity of the whole business.

But Lucy, with a true woman's tact, soon perceived how painful and dangerous this state of things was; and, taking advantage of a passing incident that broke the ice anew for them, and set conversation flowing, she began to ask questions about the recent discovery; and, ere long, Guy found himself engaged in animated, rapid discourse, and Lucy listening to him with her fair lips parted in wonder and admiration of her cousin's fate, character, and conduct. And so they reached the Hall.

There they found Mr. Morgan, who had just arrived, and who said he had waited in the hope of seeing them before he went up again to the squire, from whom he had received a hurried note, sent by a special messenger on horseback. This note he placed in Guy's hands, who read,

'My dear Sir,—I cannot get rid of some very troublesome and painful suspicions regarding my son's wife. It seems to me she has known, perhaps a long while, of Phœbe's secret, and made use of it for her own special profit. Will you look into it, and try to clear the business up? You know how much the honour of my family is at stake, and will be aware that my son's feelings are to be treated as if they were mine. You will not, therefore, invite injurious gossip by your inquiries, but rather strive to do what is required without anyone having the right to know or to ask why you do it.

'About the anonymous letters:—will you see Joshua, and judge for yourself whether you think he wrote the second one? If he confesses that, there is then, I imagine, an end to the matter; and

I shall have to own handsomely that I have wronged her, and try to make her full amends; but if he did not—well, I know what you will think then, for I saw you were surprised and suspicious yourself when you first heard her statement. Lose no time, and so oblige,

'Yours sincerely,

'GODFREY DALRYMPLE.'

Guy's first emotion on reading this was not connected with his own humiliation and suffering to have a wife who could thus be suspected; it was simply an intolerable sense of shame that Lucy should be by his side while he had to read the letter. Of Susanna—for her own sake—he scarcely thought; of his own married future he was reckless; but the sight of this letter seemed to burn like caustic into his soul when he saw its terrible suspicions reflected back, as it were, upon him with tenfold force in Lucy's anxious and inquisitive look, who saw his trouble without knowing or guessing the reasons.

But the sound of Guy's voice, as it became

suddenly harsh and constrained, warned her of some danger or distress in which she felt instinctively she could not be permitted to share.

'Yes,' he said to Mr. Morgan, 'do exactly as my father suggests; only, while you guard *others*, do not mind me.'

'Others! Who were they?' asked Lucy of herself; but could get no satisfactory answer.

'May I speak to you for a moment?' said Mr. Morgan; and Guy, in answer, went apart with him a few paces, leaving Lucy standing alone in the Hall. Then Mr. Morgan said, in a low voice,

'Instead of going home, I went to the sexton's. I have seen him, and am satisfied he did not write the letter received by your wife.'

'*If* she received it,' corrected Guy, in the same low tone.

'True, if she received it,' assented the lawyer. 'Can you get me the letter to look at?' Guy smiled, as he answered,

'I shall be surprised if I can—now.'

'You mean that—'

'That if I do not misunderstand my wife's skill and decision of character, she has destroyed it.'

' Guy ! Guy ! ' suddenly interposed Lucy, coming breathlessly towards them. ' I do believe I heard a cry just now. It sounded so like my uncle's, too.'

' No, no, my dear young lady,' said Mr. Morgan ; ' do not alarm yourself, I heard it too ; but I think it was only one of the men servants in the courtyard calling to another.'

' Shall we go ? ' said Guy, looking at Lucy, who put out her hand, had it clasped in another hand, strong, warm, and tremulous ; and so, for the second time, Guy and Lucy were passing along the corridors of Branhape, linked together, only now it was he who led the way, and she who passively and silently submitted.

And thus, too, they crossed the threshold to go into the room where the squire lay, just a few seconds only after Susanna had crossed it to go out of it, leaving behind her the lord of Branhape stark and still.   '

' Let us enter gently,' whispered Guy ; ' he may be asleep.' Thinking thus, he advanced with Lucy nearer and nearer to the prostrate form, till suddenly there burst from him a wild, inarticulate cry, Lucy's hand was dropped, he rushed forward, took up the clay-cold hand of his father, gazed in his face, kissed his lips passionately, and dropped by his side, no word spoken.

And Lucy also, forgetting Guy and everything else in the world, when she heard the sudden wail of anguish, and understanding only too well what it meant, burst into passionate weeping as she knelt on the other side, crying,

'O my uncle! my own dear, dear uncle!'

But her increasing distress at last roused Guy. He rose from his knees, and went round to where Lucy was still sobbing away her very life, making Guy's blood curdle as he heard for the first time a woman's hysteric laugh. He put his hand upon her shoulder, but she did not notice it. He compelled her to look round on him, but the sight of his face only brought back new consciousness of the terrible shock she had sustained. He took her hand, and turned to lead her from the chamber; and behind the screen he found Mr. Morgan and Mrs.

Hammett, who had followed them, and of course knew all.

'Wait here for me,' said Guy, in a hollow voice, to the lawyer. He passed on with Lucy into the corridor, and turned.

'That is my room,' whispered Lucy, pointing in the opposite direction.

'No, no; never more! *She* is there!—my wife.'

Guy took her to Mrs. Hammett, and said—

'Mrs. Hammett, I trust my cousin with you. You will guard her, I know.'

'I will.'

'You will not leave her under any circumstances?'

'No—no; trust me.'

Guy said no more to either of them, but returned to the drawing-room, where he found Mr. Morgan standing near the window busily engaged with some book that he appeared to be intently studying, but which he put away in his pocket as soon as he heard Guy's voice, and which he forgot altogether when he heard the first few words addressed to him.'

'Have you looked at my father?'

' Yes.'

' Are you satisfied he died naturally?'

'You mean—' said Mr. Morgan, hesitatingly, for the apparent meaning was too terrible to be received without scruple.

'Mr. Morgan, I must say a few words about myself—and—my wife. In spite of many facts that I did not quite understand, I have always had faith in her substantial honesty as well as in her affection for me. You will perceive that it could hardly be otherwise; we have known each other, or at least have had the fullest opportunities of knowing each other, from childhood. When I became engaged to her I felt myself under a new bond of honour and good feeling, both of which called on me to reject unworthy suspicions. I did reject them. I gave her my faith. And now that I find my faith beginning to shake it is far from impossible I may err on the other side, and do her actual injustice. Guard me from that! I say guard me; for, standing here by my dead father's body and in the sight of Heaven, I tell you terrible fears are in my heart. I left him only three hours ago better, and expecting one whom he loved so dearly that the very thought of her coming was enough to have kept him alive till she came, even if death had successfully stricken him a moment after. Yes, sir, I left my father thus, and I left my wife there.' Guy pointed as he spoke in the direction of the cabinet, little suspecting that he might then, if his vision had been strong enough, have detected the gleam of an eye fixed upon him through the very wall he looked at, and which was half-divining by his look and gesture what he must be saying.

Mr. Morgan answered nothing for a minute or so. He turned away from Guy's inquiring gaze; went again to the squire's lifeless body; seemed to study him all over; took up one of the stiff hands and felt the fingers, took up the other hand, which was closely shut; tried in vain to make the fingers relax their hold, but suddenly saw something appearing from within the palm. He called then to Guy,

'Do you see that?'

'Yes; it is the end of a folded bit of paper,' responded Guy.

' Can you extricate it from the hand ? '

Guy did so with some difficulty, and then read aloud in agitated tones to himself and the lawyer the following words, hastily scribbled in pencil by the squire's hand :—

' MY DEAR BOY,—You *must* know what I have now to tell you before you again see your wife. Robert will wait with this in the Hall to watch your coming. The following is a copy, from memory, that I have just made of an inscription you will find in your mother's Bible, written by Phœbe :—

'Susanna knows all. In case I should not have the courage to confess what I have done before I die, and to right those that I have wronged, I have told her all, that she—

There the writing suddenly ceased.

The two men looked upon one another with blanched faces, though beneath the awe in Guy's look there was a something terrible.

' Well, has she murdered him ? ' he said at last, in a voice of measured distinctness.

'No, no; I do not think we must allow ourselves to leap to such frightful conclusions.'

'You see this writing; you know her motives; and there is my father. And Lucy—O God! why she heard his dying cry?'

'Nay, nay, my dear sir, you are a young man; you are naturally excited at the loss of so inestimable a father almost as soon as you have found him, and at the deception practised on you by your wife, which I own to be perfectly inexcusable.'

'Oh, you think so?' said Guy with bitter irony. 'But you do not know what an idiot she had to practise upon, or you would see some excuse for her. You will not easily understand that, I think.'

'Where is—is this young lady?' And it was noticeable that from that time Mr. Morgan never again used the word wife to Guy.

'Probably watching us from the adjoining room.'

Guy said this, not as believing it, but as simply trying to throw off the ever-increasing burden of his shame that he should have been the victim of a woman proved to be so infamous. But Mr. Morgan, taking his words literally, went in the direction indicated and peered anxiously over the surface of the wall. There was a gleam of some kind of reflected light visible to him for a moment, and then it disappeared, and quite another kind of light was perceptible shining through the wall. There was, then, a hole there. Mr. Morgan thought the sudden change might be accidental, and not what it seemed to be; but he returned to Guy, and said,

'I can now tell you something more; only do not again excite yourself or me, for I wish to be of service to you for your father's sake. She has been here since he wrote this, and probably it was her coming stopped him, for the inscription is no longer in the Bible.'

He then, taking the Bible from his pocket, showed Guy the blank inner side of the cover, as he continued,

'It was this I was looking at when you came in, and I thought I did not recollect these imperfect traces of writing as being here when I looked at

the book in the young lady's presence last night.
Now all is explained.'

' Again I ask you, has she not murdered him ? '

' I must reply, no. It is too horrible to be believed. It is so unlikely, too, for one of her sex,
and age, and appearance.'

' Yes, I said in the workshop, when I began to
suspect her, she is a most beautiful devil.'

' Suppose I go to her, and see how she behaves.'

' Very well. I will wait here.'

CHAPTER XVIII.

MR. MORGAN tapped lightly at the door of the
room where he understood Susanna was, and, ob-
taining no answer, turned the handle and went in.
It was quite an engaging sight he looked upon.
Susanna appeared in the white and gold arm-
chair, one of her elbows resting upon an elbow
of the chair, and propping up her fair face and
head, with the fingers spanning the chin, while the
other hand and arm were drooping low by her side.
The bridal-wreath once more environed the light-
coloured and beautiful hair. 'Can this lovely
creature be guilty?' Mr. Morgan asked himself, and
he replied, 'Impossible!'

But he thought while she slept he would satisfy
himself about a little question that remained on his
mind—'Had the young lady been using her room

to-day as a place of outlook?' He peered curiously
about, not at first noticing the door of the cabinet.
But when he found that, and began to put profane
fingers upon its fastening, the gentle sleeper became
disturbed,—troubled, perhaps by uneasy dreams;
and Mr. Morgan, noticing her movements, returned, and met her newly-opening eyes.

How they stared upon him! How full of wonder
they seemed! ay, even into the very farthest parts
of their blue depths! At the same time a little
colour appeared on her cheek, and a certain ner-
vousness shook the red line of lip.

'Do not be alarmed, young lady. No, pray
keep your seat, and allow me to take a chair by
your side. I am here quite in a friendly way, on
the part of Mr. Guy Dalrymple, to try to clear up
some matters that greatly trouble him. But first
allow me to ask whether you have heard the news?'

'The news,' said Susanna, with quite an air of
pretty wonder. 'No, I have not, indeed. I have
heard nothing for many hours, though I have been
expecting every minute for some time the return
of my husband and his cousin, Miss Lucy.'

'Not heard of the death of the squire, in the adjoining room?'

Susanna's answer was a scream, then a flow of passionate tears; and then she leaped up, crying aloud with great vehemence, 'Oh I must see him! My own dear father! Oh, what will my husband say? Where is he? Oh, this cannot be true!'

'It is true; and I request you to sit down, and answer me calmly a few questions.'

'Oh, I cannot—I cannot talk now! Have you no feeling? Let me go to him.'

Mr. Morgan took her hand—very respectfully as to the mode, but very firmly as to the effect—and almost compelled her to sit down again and face him, while he put questions to her that she seemed to hear instinctively and to shudder at before they had left his lips.

'Have you seen the squire since his son left him to fetch Miss Lucy Dalrymple?'

'O dear, no! Of course not. How could I, unless he had sent for me, which he did not?'

'Will you permit me to look into the cabinet yonder?'

'Certainly, but —'

Mr. Morgan did not wait to investigate the meaning of the 'but;' he went to the cabinet, got into it with some difficulty, and saw the hole he had noticed on the other side of the wall. He put his eye to it for a single instant, then turned and said dryly to Susanna,

'If you have not yet seen the squire you can see him, I perceive, very well from here.'

'I will thank you, sir, to remember who I am,' now exclaimed Susanna, reddening, though her face was altogether a strange mixture of pale and glowing tints, inharmoniously crossing and chequering one another.

'I assure you it is impossible to forget that in this house, or in your presence.'   Not knowing exactly whether this was meant as a compliment, or as something very much the reverse, Susanna remained silent, preparing for the next blow to fall, and trying to anticipate it.

'I have seen Joshua Darkley, and he has convinced me he did not write the anonymous letter you received under such critical circumstances, and at so critical a time last night.'

'Well, sir, he does not dare to insinuate that I wrote it, does he?'

'Certainly not, but I think if you will permit me to look at it and let me have it in my custody for a short time, that I may be able to discover the writer.'

'Indeed! Could you? Oh, I am so sorry, then, that I destroyed it.'

'It is destroyed, is it?' asked Mr. Morgan, looking at her penetratingly.

'Yes; I thought it was useless keeping it. What did it matter, and what does it matter? I am sick of all this coil and cavil about nothing.'

'Can you help me to decipher the inscription in this Bible?' asked Mr. Morgan, still with his cold, grey eye fastened upon Susanna's eye, which felt fascinated by the expression and the metallic lustre that every now and then flashed in it.

'N—o,' responded Susanna, faintly.

'Can you by the help of this?' And the lawyer

then placed in her hands the scrap of paper referred
to in the preceding chapter as containing the squire's
imperfect copy of Phœbe's confession.   He saw the
blue eyes dart over the whole of the writing and
drink in its meaning at a single glance, and then he
saw something so sinister in their next gaze at him
that he grew uncomfortable, and he said to himself,
almost with a feeling of alarm, mingled with his
sense of derision, 'Does she mean to make away
with me?'   But, while he rejected the thought that
had so startled him, he felt assured, by that momentary look, that this beautiful young lady was capable
of things that he did not venture to name to her;
and he began to wonder, for the first time with real
earnestness, whether she had indeed silenced the
old man in the critical moment of discovery of her
fraud.

When Susanna had slowly read the paper through,
he looked at her, and she looked at him in silence.
Then, with a smile, she handed it back to him,
saying, in her most fascinating manner, and with a
certain half-wanton languish in them, mingled with
a kind of tenderness and reproach that were inex-

pressibly moving, and which did, for a moment, dazzle the beholder,

'And is it possible I am suspected of such monstrous deception? I cannot answer this. It is too much.'

And then tears came, and she bent her beautiful head and wept. When she lifted her head a few seconds later, wondering she was not again spoken to, the lawyer was gone!

Susanna instantly rose up to her full height, gazed furtively all round to be sure she was alone, then murmured,

'I must face them. I must not seem to fear them. I will go out.'

CHAPTER XIX.

WHEN Mr. Morgan returned to the room where he had left Guy, he was surprised that he did not turn towards him, or inquire, by word or look, what had been the results of his interview with Susanna. He was standing by his father's couch, with his arms folded, and his head sunk on his breast. Two things struck the lawyer: Guy had not only moved the lamp along the table nearer to the squire's body, but he had obtained a candle, as if to institute some very close investigation. But whatever his thought, the scrutiny was over, and the candle set down on the table's edge, as if by a hand that had blindly felt for a place. When the lawyer touched him he started and turned round a white agonized face.

'Well, what have you discovered?' he asked in a scarcely audible voice.

'Nothing,' answered the lawyer.

'No, it seems to me that it is I who have made the discovery. What say you, Mr. Morgan, to these?'

Stooping down over the dead man, Mr. Morgan saw three small, faint marks upon the throat. They had either escaped him on his first examination under the imperfect light, or they had deepened in colour during the last few minutes. It was some time before he dared lift his head again, and meet Guy's wild, questioning eyes. When he did he was almost as pale as Guy himself. Guy met his look of silent and fearful confirmation with a short sharp cry of pain, and sank into a chair, burying his face in his hands.

He sat there motionless, while the lawyer silently paced the room, and minute after minute of the bridal night went by.

When at last Guy lifted his head from his hands there was a wild, fixed, resolute expression in his eyes which alarmed the lawyer more than the most passionate outburst could have done.

'My young friend,' he said, laying his hand upon his shoulder, 'this is a terrible night, but men have kept their senses under even greater calamities than these. Keep yours, that you may think and decide with me how we must act; keep them, my dear sir, if only for the sake of your cousin. Come, we must talk things calmly over—we must think.'

Guy looked up to him with a glance that made him shiver. 'I have thought,' he answered, in a low voice, 'and I see how to act to the very end of all.'

'That is well,' said Mr. Morgan, soothingly; 'suppose we talk over what you have been thinking.'

Guy shook his head.

'But, my dear sir, this is a time when it requires more than one man's brains to decide for the best.

'I tell you,' said Guy, rising and speaking slowly, 'I have decided—I have decided everything.'

'Well, will you not tell me what your decision is?'

'No; I will tell you what to do, if you will do it.'

'If it is for your good I will do it—if not, I tell

you plainly I shall refuse. What are you ringing the bell for?'

'To order a carriage to take her away.'

'Whom? your wife?'

'My wife—my bride, Susanna—send *her* away! O no.'

A scared-looking and trembling servant appeared at the door.'

'Let a carriage be got ready directly for Miss Dalrymple.'

'Stop sir,' said the lawyer, while the servant stood gazing from one to the other in amazement. 'Why such haste—you may have to consult with your cousin, her presence may be of vital importance.

'Am I master here?' said Guy looking at the servant, and pointing to the door, with his eyes still full of that blind immovable purpose which Mr. Morgan had seen gathering in them for the last half hour. 'Go, get the carriage, place her trunks upon it, let there be no delay.'

The man bowed and went out. Then Guy turned to Mr. Morgan and took his hand and said,

' Mr. Morgan, be a friend to me now: Oh ! be a true friend and take her away gently, and see her to her home. Do this for me—do it for his, for my father's sake.'

' A friend indeed I wish to be to you both,' said Morgan. ' But consider she is delicate, and is already weary with travelling, and broken down by these terrible shocks. Let her get some hours' rest, at all events.'

' She must go at once—at once,' Guy repeated in the same quick, resolute tone.

' It is snowing heavily.'

' Is it ? It will not hurt her in the carriage.'

' Guy, your cousin must not go to-night.'

' My cousin shall go to-night.' And he looked at him again fixedly, with eyes full of strong, stubborn resolution.

' The roads are in a dreadful state.'

' They will be better than down-beds in this house to-night.'

' And she, ill as she is, to have to stay at that wretched inn.'

' Mr. Morgan, thwart me no more. I tell you

she had better be in a charnel-house than here
to-night.'

'Guy Dalrymple, what means this?'

'Mr. Morgan, do this for me, I beg, I implore
you—be gentle and kind with her, but be firm.   Get
her away from here.   Don't let her see me again.
Don't let her see me now, or I should feel—'

'Well?'

'O God! as Cain might, had an angel seen him
with his knife in Abel's heart.   Take her away—
pity me, Mr. Morgan, and take her away.'

'I shall not go.'

'You will not?'

'No; your last sentence decides me.'

'Why?'

'That woman is not safe with you.'

Guy looked at him, and smiled a strange wan
smile.

'If that is your fear, go in peace.   Don't heed
what I said.   I was mad when you thwarted me,
but do not fear.   I swear to you, on the honour—I
suppose I may say of a gentleman, may I not?—I
swear to you my wife is as safe from me as if all her

favourite vices—falsehood, treachery, deceit, *murder*
—had come out of hell in their own persons to defend her.'

'Then,' said Mr. Morgan, laying both hands on
Guy's shoulders, 'then it is you who are not safe?'

He looked into his face searchingly, but Guy returned his gaze without flinching.

'Trust me, Mr. Morgan,' he said in a broken
voice. 'Take Lucy away, and when you return,
trust me you will find I have acted for the best.'

Mr. Morgan turned away, and walked to the
window, seemingly to consent to Guy's request.
But the lawyer also had formed a resolution. He
would go away with Lucy, but to what place remained to be seen. Perhaps only to a neighbouring
magistrate's and friend of Mr. Dalrymple, there to
unburden himself of his doubts about Guy's bride,
and seek counsel and assistance.

'Very well,' he said. 'I will seek your
cousin, and see if she is able to go.'

When he had gone, Guy went and stood beside
the couch again.

His face was wonderfully calm, almost as calm as

that of the dead. There was no horror in it now—
no rage, no grief. Blent with its look of wilful
purpose was a look almost of satisfaction. It was
not the look with which the young and strong usually
regard the face of the dead-beloved—the hopeless,
wistful look, which seems to say, 'Thou art very far.
When may I hope to see thee more?' It was rather
the prophetic and calm gaze of a dying man at the
dead one—the gaze which says, 'I am near thee!
I approach.'

What meant such a look on Guy's young face
this night—this bridal night?

Several times, as he heard the bustle of the men
below, as they got ready the carriage, several times
he went half-way to the window, then checked himself, and returned to the couch, with his face more
hard and resolute than ever.

'My dear sir!' exclaimed the lawyer, entering
hurriedly, ' your cousin cannot go to-night. She is
lying on the floor in a half-fainting state. Mrs.
Hammett fears she too shares in our suspicions—she
begs she may stay near you.'

Guy looked at him in silence for a minute, then

drew his palms across his eyes with a heavy sigh, almost a groan.

'Must I go myself?' he said. 'You might have spared me this, Mr. Morgan.'

'Listen to me,' pleaded the lawyer. 'Your cousin—'

Before he could finish the sentence, his wrist was seized, his arm thrust aside, and Guy was descending the stairs. The lawyer followed him down till he stopped before the door of the room wherein Lucy lay. He saw Guy push Mrs. Hammett aside as he entered.

Lucy was not quite insensible. She was lying on the carpet, with her head on a large cushion that Mrs. Hammett had placed under it. Her head was thrown back, and she drew long, difficult breath through her parted lips. Her face was white as the lace at her bosom, and her beautiful eyes were full of tears. She looked so fair, so panic-stricken and helpless, that the lawyer made sure Guy would be moved in his determination.

But whatever Guy's heart may have suffered, his will remained unshakened. He knelt down beside her, slid his arm under her, and so raised her to her feet.

'Give me that,' he said, pointing to a cloak. It was impossible to disobey his tone and gesture. Mrs. Hammett gave him the cloak, and then, while he held the half-fainting girl in one arm, he wrapped it round her. Once she threw it off, and struggled in his arms.

'Guy, dear Guy,' she cried, bursting into a wild hysterical scream. 'Speak to me! Don't send me away, speak; oh, speak to me!'

The sound of her voice and laughter, and the sight of her tears, and the beseeching caresses of her little hands upon his arms made Guy's face whiter, and his eyes more wild and full of misery.

He folded the cloak round her with the patient firmness and gentleness of a mother. Then he lifted her in his arms, and motioning the lawyer to precede him with a light, bore her from the room and down the stairs.

A gust of cold air blowing through the hall door revived and brought a sudden consciousness upon her—and she ceased to struggle while looking up at his blank, stormy eyes. He bore her out and lifted her into the carriage, at the door of which Mr. Morgan was standing, bare-headed, regardless of the snow, the sleet, and the darkness.

Guy had put her into the carriage, and was about to withdraw his arms, when Lucy, moved by a tender childish impulse, put her hands round his neck, and he felt her cold, wet cheek touch his.

' Do not mind for me, Guy—you have enough to bear without thinking of me. You should have let me stay. I would have been strong soon, and helped, not troubled, you; but now to leave you! Oh, I fear, I fear!'

Guy did not give his cousin one farewell kiss— he did not press the clinging little hands as he drew them from his neck and wrapt them in the cloak, all in that same mechanical way. Lucy leant back and closed her eyes.

Her heart could not just then question whether it might be right or wrong to love Guy. It only felt that it had sought his love and been denied; and it sank within her, smitten by a keen and bitter anguish. His great trouble filled his soul. She felt,

—'I am cast out. I am nothing to him!' She closed her eyes. She wished he would leave her, and not keep near arranging her dress and seeing to her comforts with that hard kindness and gentleness. A shawl was on the opposite seat. Guy took it, and wrapped her feet in it. Then he left her, she thought. But no, for while she weeps quietly and bitterly in the dark corner of the carriage, she suddenly feels the trembling hands at her feet again. They tighten round them, holding them in strong embrace against a heaving chest, and Guy, kneeling on the carriage steps, bows down his head, burying his face in her dress, and mingling with his strong smothered sobs, comes the passionate call on that name which the good and the wicked alike find on their lips in their hour of danger and anguish, 'My God! my God!'

The lover whose mistress holds his fate utters all his misery and love in the passionate repetition of her name, but for the poor wretch whose wounds are past all human remedy, no name has any meaning save that which Guy cried at this bitter hour, 'My God! my God!'

They parted; the lawyer entered the carriage. A moment more, and Guy stood alone in front of his house.

'Which am I?' he asked himself, with a strange smile; 'a widower or a bridegroom?'

CHAPTER XX.

GUY went back to where his father lay, and stood beside him with folded arms, thinking. He had remained thus several minutes when something attracted his eye, and made him reach the candle from the table, and bend down over the dead form. The three dark marks had become still more plainly visible.

Guy's white lip quivered with something like a smile.

'It reminds me,' he said softly, 'it reminds me my bride is waiting.'

He set the candle down, and left the room, closing the door gently.

In the passage he met Mrs. Hammett, looking scared and haggard.

'Where is my wife?' asked Guy.

'In there, I think,' the housekeeper answered, with a shudder, pointing to the door of the picture-gallery.

Guy went and stood at the door, and looked in—looked from end to end of the brilliantly-lighted room with his wild bloodshot eyes.

Susanna was there. She had replaced her bridal-wreath, and her veil was thrown back over her glittering dress. She did not see him. She was standing with her back towards the door, looking up at the pictures. She was evidently entranced—dazzled by the glitter of the frames reposing on the crimson-velveted panels. At last, moved by an irresistible impulse, she extended her long bare white arms, and, looking up and down the wall, uttered, in a low, exultant voice, the same words over and over again,

'Mine! mine! mine!'

Guy looked at her long and fixedly. At last he went into the room. Susanna turned, and, after darting at his face a sharp, searching glance, fled to him with an exclamation of joy—

'Guy, dearest Guy, at last!'

He did not push her off; nor did he bend or yield in anyway to her embrace. He stood looking down on her beautiful head, as she leant it against his shoulder.

' Are you happy, Susanna? Have you all you wish?'

' Oh, Guy! how can you ask me? How could I be happy when he lies there dead; and when everyone has been so unkind to me?'

' Unkind! who has been unkind to you, Susanna?'

' Everybody. Your cousin, whom I met, turned away from me.'

' My cousin is gone. Is there anything else you wish?'

' That lawyer.'

' He, too, is gone.'

' The servants are so disrespectful.'

' They shall be spoken to.'

' Dear Guy!'

' Is there anything more you can mention? I want to see you happy to-night, Susanna — perfectly happy. I want you to enjoy to the fullest extent all that you have endured so much for.'

Again the quick, keen glance sought his face, but she could read nothing there that she understood.

' Well, have you not, Susanna—have you not had to go through a great deal to-night?'

' I have; Heaven knows I have!'

There was a ring of truth in her voice as she said this.

' Well, let me repay you for all,' said Guy, in a low tone. ' I will speak to these servants—they *shall* obey you. As for me, I will join you in a few minutes, to leave you no more until you send me away yourself. Ask me what you will, Susanna. I wish you to be happy this night—I wish you to realize all your dreams of happiness.

' Happy!' cried Susanna, standing before him with clasped hands and flashing eyes, and her whole frame quivering with triumph, ' Guy, you said, I had borne much this night. I *have!* Heaven knows I have!' the ring of truth was in her voice still; ' but, Guy, I would do—I would bear not this again, but thrice, thrice what I have done and borne to-night, to be—'

She looked round at the splendid Hall too much excited for speech.

' To be the lady of Branhape,' said Guy, looking at her fixedly ; ' Susanna, I believe it.'

' O no! O no!' she cried, throwing herself upon his breast, ' to be your wife.'

' Do you love me then, Susanna ? '

' I do! I do! '

There was real passion in her voice and in her lovely glowing face. Guy looked down upon her and thought of those dark little marks upon his father's throat, and said,

' I am glad of that, Susanna, I am glad you love me.'

' How could you ever doubt it ? '

' Susanna! You are wondrous fair ? On my soul, I believe you are more fair than anything on earth or in heaven ! '

' Oh, my husband! that is sweet! tell me that again. Tell me I am more beautiful than Lucy ! Tell it me—I long to hear you tell me that—I

thirst for it, Guy! Oh, sweet Guy, tell me that!—
Tell me I am more beautiful than Lucy!'

'You are, indeed, Susanna. She has but a
womanly beauty, *you* have the beauty of a—! Well,
Susanna, I am glad you love me.'

He strode across the room towards the bell-rope,
Susanna clinging to his shoulder with her radiant
face thrown back and her long dress trailing on the
floor.

She laughed aloud as he dragged at the bell
rope with increasing violence.

'How the fools will run!' she said.

A little group already stood trembling at the
door—but Guy continued ringing.

'Let every servant in the house come here,' said
he.

'That old housekeeper too,' said Susanna; 'she
is the most insolent of all.'

In a few minutes the whole house was alarmed.
Mrs. Hammett and every servant in the establish-
ment came running to the picture gallery.

When Susanna saw them all assembled, she stood
a little in advance of Guy in a commanding attitude,

with head thrown back, and her figure drawn up to its fullest height.

'My good people,' said Guy, 'you served my father faithfully, will you do the same by me?'

There was a murmur among them—a murmur of earnest protestations to Guy, accompanied by looks of intense dislike at Susanna.

'Very well, then,' continued Guy, 'that,' pointing to Susanna, 'that is my wife—the mistress of this house, and I command you to obey her—to wait upon her, hand and foot. You know this is our wedding night; light the candles in the state bedroom—take her there and wait upon her. If I do not come in less than an hour, fetch me. I shall be in the room with my father; mind, I say, fetch me.'

Susanna noticed nothing peculiar in his tone. Her head was turning giddy with triumph. She looked at her own glorious beauty in an opposite mirror; she looked at her servants, at her husband, and her heart throbbed with supreme happiness. Guy met her look, and his eyes gleamed.

'My wife,' he said; 'Susanna, is this as you wish it? Is it all complete?'

'It is! It is!' she cried, again falling on his breast, and again he received her, neither yielding nor resisting, passive as a rock, when a lovely moon-lighted wave breaks upon it with soft murmurs of love.

'Come,' he said, 'give them their orders—they wait.'

He passed out of the room, and into that wherein his father lay—locking the door after him.

CHAPTER XXI.

SUSANNA stood looking at her figure at full-length in a dressing glass in the state bedroom.

The time had not hung heavily on her hands. There were the old family jewels to examine, the court dresses of several generations to inspect and try on, and, above all, there was for her bridal night the state bedroom itself, of which her imagination never wearied ; and beyond which, her imagination found it impossible to go.

After making a maid servant try on her all the faded finery in the wardrobe she had chosen a loose white dressing gown of some Indian fabric. She thought she looked more magnificent in white than in anything else, with no colour to attract the eye but the red of her thin lip and cheek, and the

VOL. III.   X

light azure of the veins in her temples and neck, and the tawny yellow of her plenteous hair.

There were two ornaments she could not resist putting on, one was a gold bracelet in the form of a serpent, and the other a large flower of jewels. This she had fastened above her forehead, where it flashed and glittered like a star.

She stood looking at herself with a flaming wax-light on each side, waiting for the bridegroom to come, for the hour was past.

Suddenly she turns with a joyful start towards the door. She hears footsteps coming up the stairs and along the passage. Near the mirror is a quaintly fashioned seat with the royal arms graven on its back. It is very high and grand look-ing, and upon this Susanna enthrones herself; and with her glorious hair rolling down below her waist, and her jewel-star glittering above her brow, looks towards the door smiling:—she knows it is the bridegroom coming.

The outer-door of the bedroom creaks, and two women come in and draw aside the heavy curtains before the inner-door and hold them back. Now, surely he comes. No, first come two men bearing lights, who wait at the door and look back; then more heavy shuffling feet and another two come in carrying a man's body by the feet and shoulders. The blood pours from his side, and just as he is they lift him on the bed, the bridal bed.

Susanna sat staring upon them with her head stuck forward and each hand clutching an arm of her throne-like seat.

Many people were in the room, now crowding round the bed or talking in hurried whispers. Susanna's head swam. She had a vague sense of Mr. Morgan's being near her, and several gentlemen. She heard, as she might have heard in a dream the words 'Locked in with his father'—'by the couch in a pool of blood'—'the pistol in his hand.' She was conscious that her own name was mentioned—still as in a dream—and then all eyes were turned upon her. But this she could only feel, not see; her own gaze had never once moved from the figure on the bed. Presently, taking no notice of anyone around her, she slowly rose and walked to the bedside, and stood holding back the curtain with one hand and

her hair with the other. The smile that she wore
when she had turned to meet the bridegroom was
on her face still—it seemed suddenly to have frozen
there. For nearly two minutes she stood so. Then
she put her foot on the steps and set one knee on
the bed. Her eyes had become like two cold,
polished stones, and a great tear lay glittering in
the hollow of each, yet she still smiled as she looked
down upon him.

It was only when a faint noise escaped Guy's
lips that her smile died away, and then the two tears
rolled down, and she said looking piteously around—

'And this is why he asked me if I loved him!
Oh, Guy! Oh, my husband? What have you
done! What have you done?'

At the sound of her voice Guy's frame became
convulsed. He raised his head a little and looked
wildly for help.

'Take her away! Take her away!' his white
lips murmured faintly.

Susanna stretched her clasped hands beseechingly
towards him, but as she saw him sink on the pillow,
and as she felt the touch of a firm hand on her

shoulder she shrank back and slid from the bed. A hand was on each shoulder now, and she stood a prisoner between two strong men. She looked up at one of them with a frightened quivering stare, and in answer he said,—

'I arrest you for the murder of Mr. Godfrey Dalrymple.'

Then she suddenly stooped and glided between the two men like an eel, and stood panting and glaring round her at the foot of the bed. It was as if her brain had suddenly given way as she looked round and saw the finish of her work.

She standing there, robed and jewelled, the lady of Branhape; her husband dying by his own hand, which he had lifted against himself to be freed from her; the grand gentlemen, from whom she had thought to command respect and admiration, looking down upon her with disgust and horror; the poor people—her own people, she had thought to rise above and crush under her dainty heel—coming forward to lay hands on her in her own house! Her wild disordered brain showed her more than these; for, as she fixed her eyes on the bare wall, such a look of horror came over her face, that it might have been Phœbe on her death-bed that she saw and heard crying to her, in her weak, piping voice, ' Susanna ! Susanna! right those I have wronged!' It was as if she fancied the dead as well as the living whom she had injured, were coming about her to lay rough hands on her, for her pale blue eyes rolled distractedly, and she kept stretching out her hands with the palms outwards, as if she were defending herself against thousands. The touch of one of the men's hands on her shoulders seemed to madden her completely. She wrenched herself from him like a tigress, with a half-smothered shriek, gave one look round, and then turned and rushed through the women and servants, who drew back shuddering, and so out at the doorway into the wide corridor. The doors at the end leading on to the terrace stood open, they could see her distinctly as she flew along, tearing as she went the.wedding-ring from her finger, the bracelets from her arms, the jewel-flower from her long yellow hair; ay, and even shreds of her robe. Once she turned, and gave the old look over her shoulder; and then,

though not a soul had stirred to follow her, she
shrieked and flew on and on, her white slippered
feet hardly touching the polished floor. Another
instant, and the lithe tall figure stood swaying on
the top of the terrace wall, sixty feet above the
courtyard. The shrieks of fright suddenly changed
to wild piercing yells of laughter, the long white
arms were tossed into the air, and then all was still
as death ; and there was nothing to be seen but the
white line of terrace wall, and the jewels lying here
and there on the dark floor, sparkling in the moonlight.

CHAPTER XXII.

CONCLUSION.

IT was one of those pleasant days which so often come to us early in the new year, when winter seems to have fallen asleep, and spring to have stolen forth to look upon her future territories — when she has not yet manifested herself by flower or leaf, but has filled the air with sweetness and the skies with soft tints. It was nearly evening on a day like this when a workman might have been seen plodding along the foot path under the chestnut trees of Branhape Park. Judging by his attire he might have been a prosperous workman; but poverty, as if dealing with a favourite child, whom even in losing she claimed to be her own, had set hard marks upon his face which prosperity's soft hand could never rub out.

The squire's old house looked very quiet and

peaceful as Stephen Waterman approached it. The blackbirds were singing in the ivy, and the evening sun was slanting down, and there was a smell of late rain. Altogether it was looking pleasant.

He went in at the servants' door, and a silent-footed little maid took him upstairs. They paused at the door of a room at the west side of the house, far, far away from the state bed-chamber, and then the little maid knocked gently and tripped away, leaving Stephen standing there with his cap in his hand.

There was no sound of steps across the room, but the door very quietly opened, and plump white fingers grasped Stephen's horny hand, and a kind smile welcomed him.

'Come in,' said Mrs. Hammett, 'but hush! He is sleeping.'

Stephen went in and sat himself in his usual place, the very edge of the chair, near the door. This is all he has taken his long walk across the park for every evening since Guy's illness. He is never troublesome, never approaches the bed, or attempts to see Guy; never asks for anything but leave to sit

ten minutes on the edge of that chair, and stare
at the bed-curtains, and then get up and plod home
again.

Mrs. Hammett's was not the only pleasant welcome he received. A pale girl, reclining in an arm-
chair near the window, raised her head and smiled
upon him very sweetly as he entered. Then Mrs.
Hammett seated herself opposite the young lady,
and resumed her knitting.

The window was wide open, and the smell of the
rain, and the cheery blackbird's song, and the faint
evening sunshine came into the room.

Presently the stillness was broken by a heavy
sigh. Mrs. Hammett laid down her knitting, the
pale girl started and clasped her hands, and like
Stephen gazed in anxious silence at the bed-
curtains,

'Mother,' said a faint voice like, and yet unlike
Guy's.

At this call Stephen fidgeted with his cap, and
looked uncomfortable. Mrs. Hammett rose and
softly approached the bed. Lucy's lips moved in
prayer. The voice, strange as it was, and strange

as the words it spoke, was yet more natural than she had ever heard it for long, anxious weeks.

'Is Susanna out too then—and father—can't we have tea? I'm so thirsty.'

'Guy,' said Mrs. Hammett, ' do you know me?'

'Mrs. Hammett, don't trouble, ma'am; it wasn't much of a blow. The steward and I ran against each other, that's all! I—but where am I? Let me get up. I am well enough now. I was only stunned.'

'Guy,' said Mrs. Hammett, in her soft, low voice, ' give me your hand—there—now look at me. You are better now, very much better, and you must try and think quietly, try and realize all that has passed, and be yourself again. You have had great trials to go through, you know, but God has been very merciful.'

There was a long silence. The next voice that spoke was Guy's.

'Who is that man there?'

'How do you know there is a man there, Guy?'

'I know there is a man there, breathing—who is it?'

Old Waterman looked terribly frightened, and laid the back of his hand across his mouth.

'Would you like to see him?'

'Yes.'

Stephen rose and came towards the bed. Guy looked at him, then smiled, and held out his hand.

'You know him then?' asked Mrs. Hammett.

'Yes, he is my—I mean—yes, I know him.'

'And isn't it very kind of him to come and see you every day?'

'Does he come every day?'

'He does indeed.'

'Does he know—all?'

'Yes, I was at the burial,' answered Stephen on his own account.

There was another long silence. Guy spoke next.

'They've buried her then?'

'Long ago—and she's a'most forgotten now.'

'So——you've been up here every day?' Mrs. Hammett noticed that whenever the word father would once upon a time have come in, Guy held out his hand to Stephen. He had done so now.

'Ay, that he has,' she repeated.

'And you?' said Guy, turning to her with his eyes full of tears. 'And you?'

'Ay, and you,' responded Mrs. Hammett, smiling and stroking his hair. 'And are you going to say nothing about your cleverest and best nurse, who has been here night and day, and made herself just such a shadow as you are yourself?'

Guy looked at her wistfully—

'What do you mean?'

'Lucy.'

'I knew it!' cried Guy. 'Several times I have been sure of it. Where is she? She isn't gone. Mrs. Hammett, I am quite well. I *will* get up.'

'You *will* do no such thing. Lucy is better than you, and shall come to you. Come, my child!'

Stephen retired to his chair, and Mrs. Hammett left the bedside as Lucy approached.

'Lucy?'

'Yes.'

'I have dreamed many things since I have lain here. Come nearer. Did I dream that you came here one night, and held my hand and said, "Live, Guy—live for my sake!" Did I dream it, Lucy?'

'I don't think you did dream that, Guy.'

'Was it true?'

'I think it was, Guy.'

'I could not answer you then, Lucy. I heard you. I felt you near, yet there seemed to be a horrible gulf between us. Let me answer you now. Come. It was not said for pity—it was said in pure truth. Was it not, my Lucy?'

'Guy, it was. I have loved you my life through, from the very day we first met.'

As Stephen Waterman plodded homeward through the park in the twilight, among the great tree-shadows, he enjoyed his evening pipe as he had not done for many a long year.

THE END.

LONDON: PRINTED BY W. CLOWES AND SONS, STAMFORD STREET,
AND CHARING CROSS.